The
Magic
Tape

David R Morgan

Illustrations by Toby Morgan

A2Z
PRESS

The Magic Tape

This is a work of fiction.

Printed in the United States of America

A 2 Z Press LLC

PO Box 582

Deleon Springs, FL 32130

bestlittleonlinebookstore.com

sizemore3630@aol.com

440-241-3126

ISBN: 978-1-946908-63-6

DEDICATION:

To mum and dad for putting the music in me.
To Bex and Toby for keeping the music magic.
To Sue and Vicki for the songs you sang
and to Terrie for all you do.

Contents

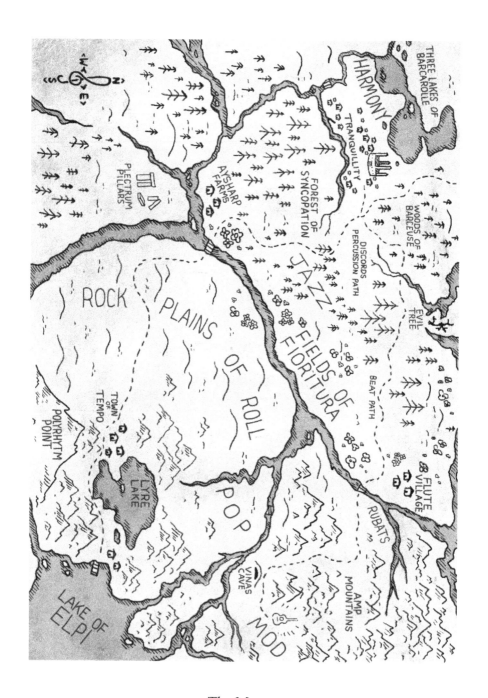

The Map

Prelude

I found this story that you are reading now as a manuscript tucked away in a red cedar violin case in my Uncle Tristan's attic.

I was searching the house after his mysterious disappearance. Beside the case were an old cassette tape player and a rather solid rectangular golden cassette tape with strange markings on it. Unfortunately, the tape player didn't work and the tape wouldn't play at all in any other device, similar or otherwise.

After much online exploring, I discovered a place that would investigate the cassette player: 'Rewind Wizard' - so I sent it away and expect its return any day. I am hoping that it will give a clue as to where my dear old Uncle Tristan has gone.

In the meantime, I found this intriguing manuscript, with its so strange story and, as you are my friend, I thought that I would like to share it with you.

Tantalisingly, the manuscript seems to be about my Uncle Tristan a long time ago, when he was young (about fifteen, it says). It is written in the third person but the handwriting and style is unmistakably that of my Uncle's and this is how it begins....

"Now what? Everything is so samey." Tristan Smith didn't realise that after this evening, nothing would ever be the same for him again.

Still, for the moment: "Now what?"

What? Well. Music of course.

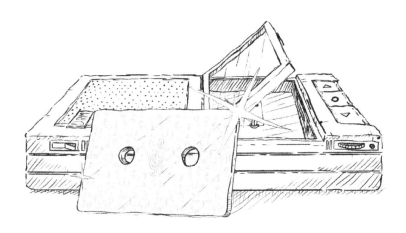

The Magic Tape

1

The Tune

If you listen silently enough, you can touch the colour of music and feel the texture of time.

Tristan Smith loved music. It touched him every way a thing can. And, it was any kind of music, any time. He loved music better than football, better than television, better than other friends, better even than chocolate; better, in fact, than anything he could think of and probably even things he couldn't. Tristan once heard, *'Music is moonlight illuminating the night. It will never hurt your feelings."*

'Ok, violin, I'll try not to hurt *your* feelings!' he thought as he picked up his violin and tried to play.

At fifteen, Tristan was a loner. Since the twins, Beatrice and Florence moved away, he didn't really have any friends. Whilst the other students were playing games, at the cinema, or going to parties, Tristan would be somewhere on his own, listening to music. He followed the lives of the great composers and musicians; like Mozart, Vaughn Williams, Beethoven, George Gershwin, and Lennon and McCartney. And, he loved music in all its forms: classical, folk, Motown, rock-n-roll, jazz, and R&B His very favorite was hard to decide but if pressed, he would have to say Vivaldi and his magical violin music.

So, inspired by Vivaldi, Tristan proudly tucked his violin under his chin and began to slide the bow across the strings in a valiant effort to teach himself to play. His music teacher, Miss Quick, said she *knew* that Tristan would really love the violin and taught him the basics, but Tristan struggled with the practice part of learning such an elegant instrument.

Thinking about his friends, the twins, now far away, Tristan sighed a little sadly as he said to himself, "Who needs friends anyway?" He smiled. His violin practice was progressing as slowly as a snail without a shell but he was determined to teach himself. Sometimes he almost made music that sounded as if he could play but most of the time the sound he made was more like scratchy fingernails on a chalkboard.

Miss Quick said, "Music comes from inside each of us and is very personal. Music cannot be hurried. So, although not very good at present, he would persevere. So far, he wasn't Vivaldi – that's for certain.

Downstairs, Mrs. Smith was growing rather worried about the fact that Tristan couldn't seem to cope without music. Tristan's father, however, whilst understanding his wife's concern, could not help being rather pleased that his son was enthusiastic about something so creative.

"Music makes his hair curl," he said. Indeed, Tristan's dark hair was very curly. He bought Tristan his own small grey and matt-black plastic cassette recorder with a built-in silver speaker. Tristan was overjoyed with the gift. It meant he would be able to listen to any music he wanted, anytime, anywhere.

Tristan took the player with him to Four Season's Park - his favorite place near his secondary school, St. Julian's. Four Season's Park stretched expansively across its many acres and was filled with trees covered with lush foliage; including willows, oaks, pines, and ash trees. There was also a lake where people rowed boats rented from an old white-haired boat keeper.

The boat keeper had been there for years. His grilled, sausage-like facial skin and piercing blue eyes made him difficult to go unnoticed. He was always watching everything around him as he talked to his boats and himself about something that no one else could quite overhear. It seemed his boats were his children and it was obvious he loved them.

Some often remarked, "Of course, he's slightly cracked."

But the old boat keeper seemed to be keenly surveying and seeing more than he would disclose. It was as if he was not only a Boat-Keeper, but a Keeper of secrets. Tristan knew that there's always more than one story about someone and other things to see beyond what any eye can first take in. Not only was the boat keeper was always watching, he seemed to be waiting for something. His eyes sparkled with an inner life and understanding.

As interesting as this was to Tristan, it was difficult because he was filled with the eerie feeling that the boat keeper always seemed to have one eye on him. Even though Tristan thought this, somehow it was curiously reassuring. It felt as if the boat keeper was a friend and not a stranger; offering friendship that needed no explanation or intrusion of personal space. This was Tristan's idea of the 'perfect friend.'

Tristan loved to hide behind a large round rose bush and a laburnum that nestled next to a laurel in the back of the boat keeper's shed. This is where he went sometimes during school time when he was annoyed by his classmates or he just wanted a special hide-away to listen to his music.

He crawled under the ample coverage of the laburnum, where he was hidden from passing eyes, and listened to his music. This didn't go entirely unnoticed at his school when he disappeared from afternoon registration.

Now, on this particular evening, before the extremely strange thing happened, Tristan had come back from the park and was upstairs in his bedroom with his music and violin whilst his parents were downstairs watching television. There was a knock on the front door. It wasn't long before there was a thump of feet coming up the stairs. Tristan's door opened.

"Someone to see you," Mr. Smith said, lighting his pipe like a threat. "Think you know what about."

"Here we go!" Tristan muttered. "I simply can't be bothered with all this bother!" Grudgingly, he switched off his tape player. 'You know it is going to be a bad day when the letters in your alphabet soup spell D-I-S-A-S-T-E-R,' he thought.

With a little cough, Mrs. Clayton, Tristan's form teacher, stepped forward out from Mr. Smith's pipe smoke. "Why haven't you been to class, Tristan?" Her voice was deceptively soft but it was like biting into a soft marshmallow with a tooth-shattering gobstopper in the middle. Tristan cringed. What could he say? It would be of about as much use as wallpapering a floor! He simply stared at her.

"Please answer Mrs. Clayton," his father said sternly as he puffed on his pipe.

Silence.

"Tristan!"

Tristan didn't want to be part of what he considered this hit-and-run conversation. He began playing his favorite Mozart tune in his mind - the music from the Magic Flute.

"No use," Mr. Smith said finally, agitated and re-filling his pipe. "Come downstairs, Mrs. Clayton. Have some tea." Then, he turned to Tristan and said, "Can't understand you, son! We'll talk about this later. Until then, you're not having this.." and he picked up Tristan's recorder, relit his pipe, and walked out of the room. The dejected school teacher followed.

From the other side of the door, Tristan could hear, "Tristan-this" and "Tristan-that." Then, silence.

He lay back on his bed, closing his eyes for a few minutes which ticked into over an hour. When he opened his eyes, it was dark. He jumped up and switched his bedside light on. His room was undisturbed and his tape player was unreturned.

Then, he saw the strange new object on his bedside table. He moved closely to look at it. The rectangular object was a beautiful golden colour and shimmered with etchings of all manner of musical notes around it. The object was the size of one of Tristan's tapes and had two holes in it exactly like a cassette. Other than that, it appeared solid.

As he picked up the golden cassette, he discovered it was heavy for its size; heavier than he first thought. He realised that it might not just *be* gold coloured. 'It might *be* real gold!' Tristan pondered. 'But how could it have gotten here? His father couldn't have put it there? Why would he give him a present, let alone such a curious one?'

Suddenly, there was a thump of footsteps. Tristan smelled the aromatic odour of pipe tobacco. The handle of his door started turning. Quickly, Tristan slipped the golden object into the pocket of his jeans. His father strode in with a firmly set frown on his face.

"Now son, what's this all about, eh?" He took his pipe purposefully out of his mouth.

Severe silence.

"Tristan," his father began. Tristan knew he was angry because that was the only time he used his full name. "Tristan, I'm asking you, what's wrong? Your mother and I are worried about you. What's going on?"

"Look, honestly, Dad, it's nothing." Tristan forced a reply. "I'm doing nothing."

"I know and it's the way you're doing 'nothing' that's so annoying. Why are you missing classes?"

Once more....silence.

"Right, wiseacre," his father growled. "You're in a hopeless mood and I'm tired. Go to bed straight away. We'll talk tomorrow!" With that, smoke billowing, he waited outside as Tristan undressed and got into bed. "No music until you explain," he said firmly and, switching off the light, he left, closing the door with soft rebuke.

As soon as the door shut, Tristan retrieved the mysterious object from his jeans. It glowed in the dark as if some inner light was attempting to burst out.

'If only I had my tape player.' He was sure that it was some type of cassette. 'What music would it play?' he wondered. Oh, his beloved music; his huge release of stress. To Tristan, life without music seemed a bit of a mistake. Without his melodic soundtrack, life seemed totally limp and lacklustre.

Biting his top lip, he determined he would search for his tape player after his parents went to bed.

At last, the landing light, visible through the crack at the bottom of his door, went out. He heard his parents' bedroom door close, the last whiff of tobacco faded away.

On cat-toes, Tristan crept downstairs to his father's study. Usually, it was out-of-bounds but tonight was special. Carefully, he opened the door. There, on his father's paper-strewn desk, he saw his recorder.

He tip-toed towards the desk and, ejecting the tape that was already in the machine, compared it with the golden object. It was exactly the same size! Remarkable! Too remarkable to be merely coincidence? Perhaps!

Then, much to his surprise, Tristan felt the object pulling itself towards the player. The strength of the attraction grew greater with each passing moment, pulling more and more vigorously. This was remarkable!

The tape clicked neatly in! Tristan closed the cover and, turning the volume down low so that not too much sound would be made, he switched his player on...nothing! Nothing!

No…..like one ghostly vibrato of a phantom mandolin, strange music started playing like a wonderfully scented wind on a warm close day. Then, it grew into the most enchanting tune Tristan had ever experienced. It didn't seem to be coming so much from his machine but, rather, from deep inside his body; threading and weaving, filling all his senses and carrying him away like a dream.

He gazed around. Somehow, the study appeared to be growing fainter and fainter like an umbered photograph fading, dissolving in liquid; parts of the study stretched and began to vanish away. The thoughts kept going over in his mind as he listened to the enchanting music, '*Life seems to make sense when I am filled with music. Without it - terrifying chaos. A world without music – unimaginable.*'

The marvellous music grew stronger despite the fact that the player's volume stayed the same. Strange music, created by instruments he could not imagine, transported him away. Another room was becoming distinct from underneath the now rapidly dissolving surface of his father's study like a television picture fading out as another was brought up into focus.

He was definitely somewhere else! Tristan was just about to see where he was going when, with a loud 'CLICK,' the music ended.

He was back in the study. Things were as clear as clear could be. His father, cross and rather pale, was standing in front of him with his finger still on the machine 'off' switch.

"For goodness sake, Tristan, what the devil are you doing?" His father was bleary eyed. "You woke us with those strange sounds. It's getting very late!"

"I...I just wanted to hear some music," Tristan answered nervously.

"What! Stuff and nonsense! If you ever, I mean ever, do this again, I shall confiscate your player for good!"

7

Angrily, he picked up a pipe lying in an ashtray and, with great agitation, felt to see if it contained tobacco. Finding it did, he lit it. Go to bed!" he commanded. "I'll talk to you tomorrow."

Strange music started playing like a
wonderfully scented wind on a warm, close day.
Then, it grew into the most enchanting
tune Tristan had ever experienced.

2

The Tune's Reason

"You're going to have to snap out of it, son." Mr. Smith put his morning paper down and with determination glared at Tristan.

'Yes, I do and snap - makes me sound like a Kit-Kat!' Tristan couldn't bear to be lectured to now. The only thing he could think of was hearing the wonderful tune again and being transported to the curious ghost room. But for the sake of peace, "Yes. I know, Dad. It's just....something."

"What sort of something?" His father put his pipe down.

Silence.

Tristan thought, 'Something like... I wasn't originally going to get a brain transplant but then I changed my mind.'

Silence.

"Tristan, you're as tiresome as this pop-up toaster that refuses to pop properly!" Mother said, scraping burnt bits off a piece of toast.

"Look, I don't mean to be, you know...."

"What is it then, son?" his father asked in a trying-to-get-to-the-bottom-of-things voice.

What could he say?

"No answer, eh? Really, Tristan!" his father began sternly. "Well, I'm making sure that you go to school today. Your things ready?"

Tristan sighed, "Yes, Dad."

"Your satchel." Mr. Smith handed it to him like a warning. Tristan was loaded into his father's old Rover. Immediately, he switched on the car radio to hear some music.

"No, you don't!" His father switched it off. "No music until you stop being foolish."

'Foolish!' Tristan felt insulted and also thought, 'Foolish is as foolish does.'

At school, the lessons dragged intolerably. However, an opportunity to escape presented itself at mid-morning break. His English teacher, Mr. Lampeter, was on playground duty. Mr. Lampeter looked just like a big, overfed mole standing there in his 'Haggis-tweed' jacket, hands resting on his plump belly. His short-sighted eyes, covered with thick glasses, resembled two goldfish bowls; with a black goldfish blindly darting back and forth in each. Whilst old 'Moley' Lampeter trundled along in front, Tristan slipped away behind, running as fast as he could to reach home.

Once there, he hid behind the old Scots Pine at the side of his house and peered through the study window. Empty. Turning, he saw his mother in the kitchen. 'Why wasn't she at work?' Mrs. Smith was a negotiator at an Estates Agent's. She was searching for something. She must have come home from the office to retrieve some documents.

He'd have to be extra careful. He couldn't use the doorway. So, silently and stealthily, Tristan crept through the opened window of the study instead. His tape player was in exactly the same place it was the night before. His heart gave a grateful skip; the golden tape was still inside. Hurriedly, he picked up the machine, climbed out the window, and was away and running.

He ran past the boating shed where the boat keeper was telling some story to boat number seven. The Keeper's watching blue eyes fixed on him and a small smile played on his lips as Tristan slid under the big laburnum in Four Season's Park. On one side, roses were flowering waxy red and white. On the other, the laurel, its big green leaves and creamy white blooms hugging each other, swayed in a gentle breeze. He gazed down at his black cassette player with its wonderful golden cargo. Excitedly, he turned on the machine. It seemed an eternity but was only an instant before the magical tune began to take hold of him once again, leading him away.

The sensation of distance began; the feeling of not being where he knew he was. The laburnum, the roses, and the laurel all began to grow fainter. They were obscured by a growing whiteness carrying with it new images never seen before. It was like a photograph developing before his eyes. The music grew stronger and stronger and even if Tristan had wanted to switch it off, he felt he would not be able to do so. It was like a living thing that grew more powerful and enchanting each instant. The image of where he was going became increasingly distinct and real. The laburnum finally disappeared altogether.

Tristan found himself sitting in a strange room… a very strange room! What an understatement! It was very wide and high. It was made of what looked like white marble and lit by what seemed to be a bright star whose dazzling rays were dulled only by the azure bell-shaped globe covering it. A 'Bell-star lit Hall' he discovered. Tapestries that were beautifully woven in rich colours depicting all varieties of known, and some unknown, musical notes hung on the walls all around the room. The colours were startling. They were almost electric in their effect as crimsons, saffrons, ambers, silvers, and jade mixed and were highlighted by filigrees of gold. Suddenly, the music stopped.

Tristan rose. 'What is this place?' He thought wonderingly.

As if in response to his silent question, a figure appeared

from behind a high-backed, bell-shaped chair. The man was tall and thin, slightly hunched and bald with long silver-blue moustaches that were so long they almost touched the floor. He wore a cassock of silver-white and about his middle was a golden chain of tiny tinkling bells.

"Wh....who are you?" Tristan asked nervously as the old man moved closer.

The old man's eyes gleamed kindly. "I am Conn Ductor," he said in a musical voice.

Tristan marvelled at his manner. Each movement was in rhythm as if in response to some soundless tune.

Turning around, the man said, "Come." He started walking and, with a wave of his hand, indicated that Tristan should follow. Tristan followed but kept a firm hold on his tape recorder. They walked through a large, bell-shaped doorway into a much smaller room. Again, this room was filled with marvellous tapestries of musical design hanging on the walls. The chairs and large white table were shaped like -

"Bells!" Tristan exclaimed. "Everything is bells!"

"To be sure!" said the man, smiling. "Sit yourself down. You have come far."

"I have?" Tristan didn't really believe what was happening.

"Indeed, Manchild!" The old man nodded, walking over to a bell-shaped fireplace. With a wave of his hand, a blazing fire rose high in the grate.

"My!" Tristan blinked with disbelief and sat down.

Conn Ductor smiled at his surprise. "My skill amazes you! Even though my power is now diminished, Manchild, I am still Conn Ductor, last of the Waltz Lords. Forgive me, but I am going to dive right in and tell you all for time is rushing by. Once there were three Waltz Lords; myself, Conn Ductor, and Inno Vator and Comm Poser. We formed a brotherhood; I balance this world called Audia that you are now in and

Inno Vator balanced your world, which we call Lumio. Thus, since the beginning, Lumio and Audia have existed side by side in different dimensions. We gave your race the power of sound and you gave ours the power of light. It is always better to light a candle and sing than scream in the darkness."

He paused and then continued, "Comm Posor, the traveller, and the third of us, connected the balance between the Spheres. However, a long time ago, now half-forgotten, an unknown evil came from the farthest corner of Audia - Chaos Desert – destroying the balance we had maintained for so long and our brotherhood was broken and both worlds weakened." He fell silent.

Tristan was about to say something when, out of a shadowy corner, came a plump little man about Tristan's height. He had short arms and legs and spiky green hair. He was dressed in trousers, a shirt, and a short jacket; all of many different colours. Suddenly, the little man's hair turned from mint-green to garish pink. Tristan gasped.

"Scherzo!" Conn Ductor said firmly. "Don't upset our guest."

"I...I'm not upset, just a little surprised." Tristan said, summoning a nervous smile.

"Conn Ductor, see, the Manchild likes me," Scherzo said, taking Tristan's hand in a vigorous shake of friendship.

"That is as may be," Conn Ductor emphasized, "But we are wasting valuable time."

"Nice to meet you, I'm sure," Tristan said.

Scherzo sat down, his hair turning purple.

Conn Ductor gazed at Tristan. "Listen!" he said, waving his left hand in an extravagant circle. "What do you hear?"

Tristan listened as hard as he could. 'What am I meant to hear?' he thought. 'All there is is silence!'

"I'm sorry, but I can't hear anything at all," Tristan said at last, slightly exasperated.

"Exactly!" Conn Ductor said sadly. Scherzo brushed a

rainbow tear from his own cheek.

"Sorry, but I don't get it!" Tristan said, "Exactly *what*?"

"Nothing!" Conn Ductor waved both hands in the air. "Exactly nothing because there is nothing to hear. Those who waltz are considered mad by those who cannot hear the music. Soon, no dancing will be possible and there will be no music anywhere. The mad silence will be so loud we won't be able to hear anything else. Yet, this is Harmony, land of the Valleys of Music, the greatest land in the Sphere of Audia. A land that should be filled with countless wondrous sounds. What is any world without music? It is a wasteland without meaning – no classical music, no rhythm and blues, no jazz, no pop, no hip-hop, no marching bands, nothing. Silence or just noise – crashing, clanging, noise!"

Then, with a serious look about him, he continued, "Manchild, I know this is difficult to take in but you must see for there is a terrible place in Audia, almost as powerful as ours, called Din, where the Discords abide. In the past, the Concords of Harmony here were always victorious and lived in harmony and splendour under the line of the Queens of Tranquility. The Discords of Din have been fighting us forever, trying to make their waves of noise drown out our beautiful music."

The old man paused and scratched his chin. Then said, "During the last Symphonic conflict, we mustered all our forces to overcome the danger from Din for all time. I called all my power into play. I kept myself disguised, for few know that I am a Waltz Lord. Secrecy these days is important! Anyway, with the final defeat of the Discords and Lord Bang Bashboom's overthrow and passing, we thought we had finally put a finish to their interference. It was not to be. Lord Loud Crashbang, the most devious of the Noise Lords, formed a plan deep in his abode in Din, the Castle Meegrain. He plotted to steal this from our city, Tranquility, Capital of Harmony. It is the one thing that would render us completely vulnerable to his onslaught – yes, he plotted to steal the great Golden Metronome."

Conn doctor continued, "Oh, Manchild, now we are without our treasured and beloved Golden Metronome. It is hidden from us and without it, Harmony will fade away and all Audia will succumb to the forces of Noise and Chaos. Even now, Lord Crashbang's army of Anxiety is gathering. If not for my remaining power, we would have already fallen to the evil one! Now, though, my power is draining - I feel it! We still have time to do good. I used much of my power sending you the Brio-Key - the magic tape to fetch you here. For only you, Manchild from Lumio, can prevent Chaos from taking hold."

"I don't understand!" It really was all a bit hard to take in. Tristan scratched his head. "How?"

"I will finish my explanation, Manchild, so things will be clearer. Long ago, my brother Comm Poser disappeared, never to be seen again. As he vanished so, the Sound Reaper, also known as Cacophony, emerged against the brotherhood. We learnt that he had destroyed Comm Poser with his evil eye. Inno Vator and I trapped Cacophony beneath a giant bell. Yet, Inno Vator received a mortal blow in the act; thus, Manchild, only I remain. Ages ago, I returned to Harmony disguised and have dwelt here ever since, guarding over the Golden Metronome. I didn't guard it well enough."

Conn Ductor continued, "Loud Crashbang had long wished to steal the Metronome, but never found a way until the wicked Inter Fearence, most learned of Discords, told him of Chaos – the Desert of Chaos that lay beyond the Mountains of Decadence. She told him of the legend of Cacophony, the Sound Reaper, who had been imprisoned long ago in Chaos beneath a giant bell by the Waltz Lords and of Cacophony's legendary power and hatred of Harmony. At once, the Noise Lord saw the solution to his problem. He sent his son, Baron Buzz Deafening with a Headache of Discords to Chaos Desert.

It took much time but once at the Golden Bell and wearing full head armour to deaden any musical sound, they raised the Bell and released Cacophony."

Conn Ductor sat down. "Must reserve my strength," he said. "There is a great task I must yet perform before you can help us, Manchild. Before noise spreads and enters your world as well forever."

"But how can I help?" asked Tristan again.

"Cacophony is a shape-changer. He can take many forms. He is a master of magic disguise and can even disguise himself in people we think are normal around us. Using his power, he entered Harmony and, taking me off guard and, at a safe distance, sent the Golden Metronome to an unknown destination in *your* Sphere, Lumio, thus stealing our main music and our power. Hence, the silence! Spreading, spreading. Soon to be flooded with a deep ocean of unbearable noise, endless and drowning us all. Hence, the nothing! Then, he returned to Din to regain his full strength and prepare with Loud Crashbang for the final overthrow of Harmony and hence the conquest of all Audia."

"So, you want me to find this....this Metronome?" Tristan asked thoughtfully.

Conn Ductor got up smiling. Scherzo sprang to his feet and shook Tristan's right hand rather too enthusiastically; both obviously concluding that Tristan's realising what his task was, meant that he had accepted it.

"It will be a most arduous task, Manchild," Conn Ductor said with utmost seriousness. Tristan was about to answer but was interrupted by the musical toll of a bell.

"Preparations have begun!" Conn Ductor stared at Scherzo whose hair turned ginger.

"What's happening now?" Tristan asked, jumping to his feet.

"No time for more explanations. I have a task to perform! You must return to your Sphere." Conn Ductor took a thin purple rod out of a bell-shaped box. "If you still wish to help us, which I beg you to, then return in twelve of your hours."

"But how do I get back home?"

"Reverse the tape," Conn Ductor said, hurrying out of the room.

Scherzo took Tristan's hand. "Return, Manchild, and be brave, you have a whole world of music to save." He released the boy's hand with a smile.

"A whole world - they don't ask much!" Tristan muttered to himself as he turned the tape over and pressed the button.

The tune filled the room, but this time it played backward. Just above the music, he heard Scherzo's friendly voice, "Listen to the songs that hide, in your tuneful inside."

'Funny thing to say!' Tristan thought.

Over the landscape of sound, green leaves emerged in front of Scherzo's face; branches instead of tapestries, sun instead of roof-beams. It must have been getting on towards late afternoon in Four Season's Park. The boat keeper was still telling his story but he paused and looked at Tristan with his knowing, electric blue eyes. "So, your journey begins," he muttered.

Not hearing, Tristan got up and ran to St. Julian's expecting it to be closed. You can imagine his surprise upon discovering that it was still mid-morning and the class whistle had just been blown. Break was ending. What had seemed to Tristan to be a matter of hours, had in fact been a matter of fifteen minutes or so! Harmony was truly a magical place!

"Business as usual, Laddie. Stop daydreaming!" Moley Lampeter exclaimed and ushered him to class.

'Daydream! Ha! If only he knew!'

Tristan was first out when the bell tolled for dismissal.

He quietly went into his house, replacing the recorder in his father's study without being noticed. He kept the magic tape with him.

"Have a good day, Tristy?" his mother, back early from work, asked in a concerned voice as Tristan strolled into the kitchen.

"Yes, wonderful, Mum." He thought perhaps he had sounded just a bit too enthusiastic. "Do you always have to kill them first?" he added, smiling at his mother who was sticking a fork into some sausages that were ready for grilling.

"You try my patience," she grinned.

"O.K, but only if you promise to try mine sometime."

After tea, Tristan's father returned his recorder to him, but first he made Tristan promise to improve his behavior in regard to what he was going to do next.

As Tristan climbed the stairs to his bedroom later, there was no doubt in his mind as to what he was going to do next.

Tristan was about to say something
when, out of a shadowy corner,
came a plump little man about Tristan's height.

3

The Task Begun

There was a pause, as if everything around him held its breath; which made the gently growing music even more captivating.

Like a painting filling itself in by numbers, the Bell-star lit Hall emerged where he had been before – clear and wonderful. Yes, this life is full of magical things, patiently waiting for our minds to grow clearer. Conn Ductor and Scherzo were waiting for him. Conn Ductor looked tired and somehow older. "Welcome, Manchild," he said. Scherzo waved cheerily.

When Tristan had fully arrived, he saw that there was a third person there – a girl! She seemed to be about his age with vibrant burnished golden hair curling about her shoulders and tumbling down over her pale blue robe almost to the floor. Her hair softly framed her face that was a radiantly pale gold, like clear water in sunlight. She was as beautiful as the music from his tape that was now fading in his ears.

"Hello!" Tristan said, staring at the girl.

"Allow me to present the Manchild from Lumio," Conn Ductor said to the girl.

"My name is Tristan."

"Manchild," Conn Ductor added, "this is Princess

Melody, daughter of Tranquil Queen Rhapsody."

"Rather young, isn't he?" Melody said to Conn Ductor, ignoring the boy.

Tristan grunted.

"Time grows short," Conn Ductor urged. "Much has been done during your absence, Manchild. Your task is now ready for the undertaking. You do still wish to continue, don't you?"

"Of course!" Tristan replied firmly, giving Princess Melody a defiant look.

Scherzo bounded up to Tristan and shook his hand as vigorously as usual.

"The Manchild must come to my mother," Princess Melody said. "He must understand the task fully."

"This way!" Conn Ductor beckoned, walking through a bell-shaped door to the right. Scherzo, Princess Melody, and a rather flustered Tristan, followed.

"Come, oh come, see what is to be done," Scherzo sang, his hair turning puce as they entered the strangest corridor that Tristan had ever seen. He thought it seemed narrow for its immense height, although fifteen people could have easily stood abreast in it. On either side there were columns of white marble that had huge bells carved in gold on top of them. The columns held up the shadowy vault of the marble roof that was embossed with all manner of gems – rubies, corals, garnets, and pink topaz – that were set in designs of musical notes. It was as if the golden bells were tolling soundless but visible tunes that spread across the width of the roof to merge in a cascade in the middle.

At the end of the corridor was a pair of massive bell doors, made of what seemed to be white gold. As they approached the doors, Conn Ductor gave a commanding wave of this hands and one door, apparently extremely heavy, opened in effortless silence.

Rose and lemon - tinted daylight poured in.

As they entered, Tristan saw that they were all standing at the top of a flight of large green and blue marble steps. There was a walled garden at the bottom.

As they walked down the steps, Tristan stared in amazement at the huge tree whose spreading branches spanned the roof of almost the entire garden. Instead of leaves, it was laden with clusters of crimson bells that tinkled enchanting tunes whenever a breeze lifted them.

Around the base of the huge tree were flowers like monstrous orchids of many different colours that displayed blooms of chime clusters. 'I just don't believe this!' Tristan thought. 'A garden composed entirely of bells and chimes!'

They walked a little way across the yard together. Then, as Tristan turned, he noticed that the building that they had just left was also in the shape of a colossal white bell. And, at equal intervals around it were three huge bands of gold with all manner of musical instruments carved in them.

Tristan was about to comment on its splendour when a tall, thick-set man strode towards them wearing blue and silver clothes displaying a number of musical designs. The motif of a white flute was stitched in the middle of his tunic. His long, navy-blue hair was strangely cut and streaked with green.

"Prince Andante!" Conn Ductor exclaimed, halting. "Allow me to present the Manchild from Lumio."

The Prince bowed in a most military manner.

"Manchild," Conn Ductor introduced, "Prince Andante from the Valley of Sonata!"

"Hello. I'm Tristan."

"He's very young," the Prince said in a deep bass voice.

"Yes, isn't he!" stressed the Princess, half smiling, half goading.

"I'm not at all," Tristan began. "After all, I'm..."

"Are you certain of the wisdom of this movement, Conn Ductor?" interrupted Prince Andante, ignoring the boy.

"Quite sure, young Concord," said Conn Ductor, annoyed that his wisdom in this matter should be doubted. "This Manchild is the chosen one. One who knows of the wonders of the worlds and who watches in Lumio has observed the Manchild and has let it be known that he has the unique ability to help us."

Tristan didn't know what he meant. Did he mean the boat-keeper, who always seemed to be watching him? No matter for now. The way Conn Ductor said this made Tristan feel very important. He gave Melody a rather pompous look. She deliberately took no notice.

"So be it!" Prince Andante said. "We must go to the Queen. The audience has been arranged. You are eagerly awaited." He turned and the four followed him through a pair of golden bell gates.

"Manchild will find the Metronome's lost power cord, and rout Anxiety's evil hoard," Scherzo said merrily, his hair turning to yellow and green polka dots.

They walked up a long avenue lined with tall trees. In between the trees with lush foliage of bell clusters were silver and golden frames supporting ivy - like plants whose petals and leaves were all of different colours and whose blooms were miniature harps and lyres. Every so often, these were punctuated by a tall statue of a man or woman, carved seemingly from a single gem of sapphires, emeralds, and lapis lazuli. 'It's all a bit much to take in,' Tristan decided.

The avenue linked the Conn Ductor's Bell building at one end to a white marble Palace of immense size and splendour at the other end. A huge statue stood in front of the Palace. Scherzo told Tristan that it had been hewn from one mighty flawless diamond ages ago. The statue was of a beautiful woman; probably a goddess. In her right hand, she held a chain of ears made from various precious gems. Her left hand was formed as if it should be holding something, yet it was empty. On her proud head was a helmet made from lapis-lazuli from which flowed strands of sapphire notes.

"This is a statue of High Queen Tranquility, the first Queen of Harmony, known as the Gem Goddess," Princess Melody said.

'Wonders never cease!' Tristan thought. 'She's actually consented to talk to me.'

"In her left hand, she once held the Golden Metronome – that has been stolen. Its loss is our downfall." Her voice had grown sorrowful.

"All is not lost, Princess. Hold a song in your heart!" Conn Ductor said encouragingly.

A white marble throne carved in the shape of two large joined ears sat beneath the statue. On top of the throne rose a golden lyre. Sitting on the throne was the most wonderful woman that Tristan had ever seen. She had torrents of burnished golden hair like Melody's. In and out of its tresses drifted the gold-paved pathways to all the fairy tales he had ever read or been told. Tristan gazed into her dark green eyes that were laden with dreams that had once been happy but were now melancholy. Her face had the same delicate luminescence as Melody's. She wore a single robe of white fur and on her head a diamond crown sparkled in the shape of a lyre.

"The magnificence which you see, is Tranquil Queen Rhapsody," Scherzo said, his hair turning vermillion.

"She's wonderful!" Tristan blushed, realizing what he said. Melody smiled at him.

"Wonder is the start of wisdom." Conn Ductor smiled.

Prince Andante halted, then bowed; as did Scherzo. Conn Ductor nodded to the Queen as Melody ran to her. The Queen kissed Melody on her forehead, then rose from the throne.

"Your Tranquil Majesty, may I present the Manchild from Lumio," Prince Andante said in a very formal fashion.

"Hello!" said Tristan nervously, not knowing how to

address a Queen.

"Welcome, Manchild," the Queen said in a musical voice. "The wise Conn Ductor has done well. He has informed you of the terrible fate that has befallen Harmony?"

"Well...." Tristan began, thinking that perhaps he had forgotten some very important details.

"Not in full, your Tranquil Majesty," Conn Ductor said.

"Our Music has been stolen," the Queen began. "Each passing moment silence perceptibly grows. The Discords of Din are so sure we are defeated, yet we do have the noble Conn Ductor."

"You have!" Conn Ductor assured.

Prince Andante seemed somewhat surprised, for it was still known to only a few who Conn Ductor really was. That he was, in fact, one of the Waltz Lords of old.

"Since the Metronome's loss, Harmony's dance is stilled," the Queen continued. "Music is but a fading memory and, as long as we are fading, all our colours are draining into the hue of dying roses. If this silence lingers for more than fourteen cycles, Manchild, then oblivion will close us in its mists. Din and Chaos shall overcome all of Audia – the beauty of music will be lost forever. Even now, we are as half-awakened creatures with only part of our former glory. Our salvation is the recovery of the Metronome," She cast a purposeful look at Conn Ductor. "And that can only be made possible if the first part of our plan has been performed. Is there no news?"

"Word shall come any moment, your Tranquil Majesty," Conn Ductor said earnestly.

Queen Rhapsody seemed as if she was about to speak once more when there was the sound of galloping hooves and a proud figure with greeny-blue hair streaked with red pulled up in front of them on a large stag. Though the man was covered in grime and dust, Tristan could make out green and gold clothes and on his tunic was a silver violin.

Grasping one of the stag's lyre antlers, he hurriedly dismounted, bowed to the warmly smiling Queen, and then strode across to Conn Ductor and spoke to him in whispers.

"What has Prince Crescendo of Binary to tell?" asked Prince Andante, slightly indignantly.

"His purpose is known to us," Queen Rhapsody assured. "Urgency requires that the fewer who know, the faster it can be performed."

After Conn Ductor and Prince Crescendo finished their exchange, Prince Crescendo re-mounted and hurriedly rode off. Conn Ductor paced towards Queen Rhapsody. "Your Tranquil Majesty, it is done," he said.

"Conn Ductor plays the first and hundredth fiddle, as well as all the ones in the middle," said Scherzo, his hair turning pink and blue chequers.

Tristan smiled.

"We must hurry." Conn Ductor signalled. "Manchild, prepare!"

"For what?" asked Tristan. "Please, don't you think you better tell me what is happening first?"

"Come!" the Queen smiled and then turned to Conn Ductor, "and Conn Ductor tell us of your success and plan and the Manchild's part in it all."

They started walking towards the Palace.

"We have gained time, Manchild," Conn Ductor began. "Whilst Cacophony was building his power and Loud Crashbang plotting in Castle Meegrain, I devised a plan. They did not realise that although they could steal the Metronome by devious means, I could still take their Interruptor. Whilst the enemy was busy plotting Harmony's destruction, I disguised Prince Crescendo as an evil-looking Discord. And, using the last of my journey-room's power, sent him to Din. Once there, he mingled with the crowds of Anxiety and, though it caused him much pain, under lapse-light's cloak he stole the Interruptor Rod from the statue of their founder, the wicked Critt Ike and replaced it with a fake."

"The Interruptor Rod!" exclaimed Prince Andante.

"Interruptor Rod?" asked Tristan.

"The Interruptor Rod, Manchild," began Conn Ductor, "is the power source of the Discords of Din. It is much the same as the Golden Metronome is the power balance of Harmony. It has already been disguised and hidden elsewhere in Audia."

"So your enemies are powerless then!" said Tristan. "So, all I have to do is to find your thing and everything will be alright!"

"No, Manchild," Conn Ductor corrected. "Cacophony, the evil Sound Reaper, Discord Demon, is as powerful as ever. Time is of the essence. I am sure that as yet he knows nothing about you, Manchild."

"That's something, I suppose," Tristan mused, not feeling too reassured.

"However, he will!" Conn Ductor emphasized, shaking a long thin finger at Tristan. "Yet, he must retrieve Din's true Interrupter to prevent the Discords fading before he can attend to you. We must use this time to our advantage, for once he has the Interruptor he will seek you out, Manchild. He is a shape-changer, changing his shape and disguising himself beyond anyone's ability to discover his true identity and his evil eye, always with him somewhere, sees many things. He also has the ability to travel to your Sphere for limited periods of time. I am sure he has caused many of the conflicts and disasters in your world though. It seems that your Race is quite skilled at causing catastrophes itself. Anyway, once he discovers the fakery, it will not be long before the search for the Interrupter begins. Thus Manchild, you must start the search for the Metronome at once. We must find the Metronome first or be at a terrible, deadly disadvantage."

"But how can I?" Tristan stressed. "My world is a very

big place, you know." He wondered just what he had let himself in for.

"The Amp Mountains of Pop are to the Southwest of Harmony," said Queen Rhapsody. "Bop Shoowah dwells there. He is the Keeper of Mod and in his tower is the vision ring of Moog that was created by my fellow Lady Electrika. In that ring, a girl or boy who has not yet reached adulthood and is of pure intent, yet is determined in mind and body, may see into your Sphere. This is why we need you so, Manchild. For, being from Lumio and loving music as much as we, you are unaffected by the Metronome's loss."

"But, I'm still not clear about all this."

"It will be made clear. When you arrive at the Tower of Mod and enter the Moog Ring, you will be able to see where the Great Golden Metronome is. Only you can do this but now you must concern yourself with time and Cacophony," Conn Ductor commanded. "Along your journey, you will be helped by friends of Harmony when you need them most. But, you will also encounter the allies of the evil one too. Be positive. A positive attitude may not solve all your problems but it will annoy enough negative people to make it worth the effort!"

'Be positive!' Tristan swallowed uneasily. He was having second thoughts about the whole risky business.

"However, I can lend a little light in the darkness," Conn Ductor continued, "Scherzo shall accompany you as a guide. I will let as much of the little remaining power I have flow into him. Even so, Manchild, if you do not find the Metronome within fourteen cycles and return it to Harmony, then he will fade along with the rest of us."

The thought of having Scherzo as a companion cheered Tristan considerably.

"Manchild," said Melody, coming close to him, "I want you to take this with you." She handed Tristan a perfectly rounded gem that was the size of a ping-pong ball and gave off a purplish light from within.

"Thanks!" Tristan said hesitantly. "But, can I ask what I do with it?"

Princess Melody gave him an impatient look. "Whenever you feel uneasy or fearful, take it in your hand and think of any music and you will be happy and brave again."

Tristan thought she was having him on. Still, thanking her again, he put it in his pocket.

"Manchild," said the Queen as she stepped forward. "Harmony's entire existence is in your hands. Are you still sure you wish to embark on this task?"

"Certainly. I am," Tristan said, forcing his mouth to form a rather panicky smile.

"Manchild," said Melody, coming close to him,
"I want you to take this with you."
She handed Tristan a perfectly rounded gem that was the size of a
ping-pong ball and gave off a purplish light from within.

4

The Forest of Syncopation

From the outside, the Palace had the appearance of a tremendous white marble drum with four tall flute-like towers rising around its sides. The main doors were in the shape of two giant ears carved from burnished gold.

"This is my home, Manchild," Melody informed Tristan as they stood inside the Palace.

"Please, call me Tristan." His father always said speaking on first name terms was a sign of friendship

"Why?" she asked.

"Why?" Tristan retorted testily. "Oh, it doesn't matter."

She fell silent. The others had gone into another part of the Palace. The hall where Tristan and Melody waited was huge and round. There were statues similar to the Gem Goddess set in the ear-shaped alcoves of the silvery-white walls. Each was carved from a single coloured precious stone.

"Who are they?" Tristan asked Melody.

"Queens of Tranquility, overseers of Harmony," Melody replied.

"Where's your father?" Tristan asked. "Why haven't I seen him?"

"Oh!" she said sadly, "Grand Prince Maestro was taken to the Dreamworld by the Guardian Lord of Spheres during the last Symphonic war."

"He passed away?"

"Yes," Melody said, "passed….."

Tristan's gaze was suddenly arrested by the sight of a tremendous circular staircase he could see through the two ear-shaped doors. The stairway seemed to wind endlessly upwards and its steps were white marble with occasional black steps, like the keys of a piano. If Tristan didn't know this was all real, he would have believed he saw it the same way Aunty Nora saw things when looking into a fire or down the old well at Patteridge. A well where she claimed many undefined forms gazed back at her. Her imagination played tricks by creating living beings out of flickering flames and hidden figures from dark water.

"Manchild," Conn Ductor beckoned as he walked across the great hall, passing the doors that concealed the piano-key staircase. Then, they walked through the door between two statues - one made of emerald, one of topaz. Tristan and Melody followed.

The high, round room they entered had golden musical columns and walls that were coloured like the sky with fluffy white clouds wandering across the blue.

Tristan quickly realised he was inside a giant birdcage. He stepped back nervously as he saw the enormous, apple-green owl-like creature sitting on a large silver perch next to him. It had two heads and a long multi-coloured peacock fan for a tail. Tristan thought it was as large as an elephant. The next moment he jumped violently as the owl creature hooted loudly.

"Hold no fear, Manchild!" Queen Rhapsody entered behind them. "This is the Royal Diatonic Fugue."

"The what?"

"The creature that will carry you to the borders of Harmony, where you will venture through the Syncopated Forest on foot to the beginning of Jazz," said Queen Rhapsody.

"You mean I've got to ride on THAT!" Tristan exclaimed, horrified.

"Yes." Conn Ductor said. "It can take you no further, alas, for once outside the safety of Harmony, you would be too easily seen in the air and simple prey for our enemies."

Suddenly, Conn Ductor placed his hand on Scherzo's head, which, for a moment, seemed to glow. When he removed his hand he sighed as if a great weariness had overcome him. Prince Andante entered, holding a jewel-encrusted cup. He handed it to Tristan. "Drink this!" he commanded.

Tristan had taken a dislike to Andante's steady military manner. He seemed the sort of person who makes you feel guilty simply for smiling and the boy was rather hesitant to drink the unknown substance.

"Come, Manchild!" Conn Ductor reassured. "After you reach Jazz you will have far to walk. You are thin enough already. And this will give you strength to begin."

Scherzo nodded vigorously in agreement, his hair changing from orange to silver. Tristan considered for a moment and then took as small a sip as possible. He could hardly believe his tongue - the liquid filled his mouth with the delicious taste of fruit and he drank it all.

"Thanks!" he said, handing it back to Prince Andante who received it with his usual stiff formality.

"You had best mount the Creature now," Conn Ductor urged.

'Oh, dear!' thought Tristan. 'I don't like the look of this at all! Moley Lampeter tried to annoy me with bird puns once, but 'toucan' play at that!'

Suddenly, Scherzo grabbed his hand saying, "When we are together, there will be nothing to fear - ever." Tristan smiled uneasily and walked up the creature with him.

"Take care, Manchild," stressed Melody.

"Yes," Tristan replied. "I'll try!" And then, with Scherzo, he mounted a small set of steps and climbed onto the saddles that were strapped onto the back of the creature. It didn't move. Tristan was surprised how soft its apple-green feathers were.

"Good luck, Manchild!" bid the Queen. "Remember, only those who risk going too far can possibly find out how far they can go. I know you can go all the way."

Tristan thought this encouraging though, somehow, he was worried at the same time.

"Be aware!" cautioned Conn Ductor and, looking at Scherzo, "Look after him, old friend. Remember what I have told you."

Scherzo nodded and his hair turned powder blue. Prince Andante gave out a commanding musical hum and the Royal Diatonic Fugue began to flap its great wings.

"Good-bye," called Tristan, but his farewell was drowned out by two loud musical warbles from the creature's beaks as it spiralled upwards and flew through an egg-shaped hole that was opening in the flute-vaulted roof. Higher and higher the owl-creature climbed like a spiralling song mounting the scale.

Tristan had never flown before. 'If Mum and Dad could see me now!' he smiled to himself. It was thrilling! The Towers of Tranquility, the Bell Building, and many other buildings that ran in line with the Avenue, like spokes in a bicycle wheel, were now but specks on a golden green cloth.

They flew fast forward over one valley, then another, then another, and another; each joined by roads through what Scherzo told Tristan were the Ritornelle Hills! Then, across the three lakes of Barcarolle and into the woods of Berceuse. Tiny towers and clusters of buildings were dotted here and there. From the air, each cluster seemed arranged in a musical pattern, like notes Tristan had seen on sheet music.

"What was the last Symphonic War like, Scherzo?" Tristan asked.

"Bang Bashboom I saw, fight High Prince Maestros in the

war. Maestros' music entered him in many places, and he made such funny faces," Scherzo said, his hair turning yellow.

'Hum, that's no answer,' thought Tristan. 'Probably doesn't want to talk about it.' Sure enough, Scherzo didn't say another word on the subject and the Creature flew on for what seemed like hours. Then, turning around, Scherzo said, smiling, "Soon, Manchild, you will see, that we shall reach the borders of Harmony."

Tristan peered down. Indeed, the land was beginning to change – it was no longer pleasant greeny-golden hills rolling away to meandering silver-blue, whistling streams, and woods of tinkling-bell trees. Below them now were closer clusters of tall, brass coloured trees with strange twisted, convoluted branches and stems that continuously emitted curious sounds.

The owl creature slowed to a hover and then circled slowly earthward. Tristan could feel his heart thumping with excitement, mingled with certain fears.

The creature hovered just above the tops of the trees that created the roof of a great dense forest.

"We'll have to chance, jumping for that branch," Scherzo said, pointing to a tree whose twisted bronze branch brushed the owl creature's wings. Tristan could see that there was no way they could land - it was too dense. On the other hand, they were still very high up and he certainly didn't fancy jumping for an object that didn't promise much safety.

"I know it's high, but you really must try," Scherzo urged, his hair turning brick red.

"Oh, dear!" Tristan moaned, submitting reluctantly. Scherzo grabbed his hand. Tristan made sure his tape-recorder was secure and, together, they jumped. Tristan closed his eyes. Like leaves caught on a soft breeze, they glided onto the branches below.

The owl-creature, still circling above them, gave out two musical warbles, then rose higher and higher; soon disappearing as it made its way back to the city of Tranquility.

"Now what?" Tristan asked. "I can't see anything below. We're so high up and these strange trees are so thick. How are we going to get down? The trunks are as smooth as brass."

"Hold my hand and close your eyes, then wait for a big surprise," Scherzo said.

'Oh, well!' thought Tristan. 'In for a penny!' And, closing his eyes, he suddenly felt himself jerked downwards. "Hey! You're pulling me off!" he cried, startled by the descent. But, when he opened his eyes, he saw his feet land light as feather down on the ground.

"Good grief!" Tristan exclaimed, very pleasantly surprised. Beneath him was a head of gentian-blue hair. Scherzo smiled.

Tristan gazed about him. The growing trees clearly stretched in all directions beyond the horizon of his sight, scratching the back of the sky. The trees were taller than any he had ever seen before, except perhaps for the Giant American Red Woods he read about in his mother's *National Geographic*. But, these trees had the colour and appearance of brass, although when touched, they felt like wood, except much smoother. The branches were contorted and whether it was just Tristan's over-active imagination or not, they gave the appearance of all manner of brass instruments; trumpets, clarinets, trombones, and saxophones. The leaves curled or funnelled like mouthpieces so that when the wind passed through them they gave off strange sounds; remarkably like the instrument-branch on which they happened to be growing.

"Lovely. Rather curious, though!" Tristan pondered, slightly dazed.

"Even whilst green sounds sing gold as the old winds blow, there lie before us ways I do not know," Scherzo said, prodding Tristan. "If we do not wish to walk blind, the Percussion Path we must find,"

"The... oh, of course!"

34

So, in the Forest of Syncopation, the two companions started searching for the Percussion Path. As they wandered, Tristan kept thinking that he saw leaves and fallen branches moving and little whisperings behind their backs; but every time he turned, all he saw was Scherzo's hair changing colour or the bronzed light of the long day percolating through the foliage. Yet, he kept an enquiring eye, always on the alert. Finally, "I know I saw something that time, Scherzo!" he said, halting.

"Jammings! Jammings! Jammings!" Scherzo chuckled.

"Pardon?"

Scherzo pointed. Tristan just managed to catch a glimpse of a small creature with black arms and legs, scurrying rapidly behind a tree and making a chattering sound that reminded Tristan of the noise of someone tap-dancing.

"What is that?" Tristan asked, amazed.

"The little happy dancing things, are the creatures called Jammings," Scherzo replied, his hair turning half-black, half-white. "They are friends of Harmony, our search will be simple now, just wait and see!"

And so saying, Scherzo went quickly up to where the little creatures had hidden itself and started making the same tap-dancing sound. In next to no time, with a chattering flurry, the two were in a circle of these little creatures, each making variations of the same sound. Scherzo appeared to be talking to them.

Each creature was approximately two to two-and-a-half feet tall. They were all black, brown, or chestnut colour in body and hair and the brightest white mouths smiled on their fluffy light-beige heads. They had white lines around their brown eyes, no nose as far as Tristan could see, and smooth light-beige hands and feet. Tristan thought that they almost looked like bizarre drumsticks come to life; as only large arms and legs appeared to move. Their bodies seemed still as stiff could be!

"Scherzo, what's happening?" Tristan couldn't understand what was going on.

Scherzo turned and scurried over to Tristan. "Good news to be had, yet, alas, also bad." His hair flushed ginger. "The Jammings will show us the straight path out, but there are Discord spies about. We must keep a keen eye and a sharp ear, if we are to get safely out of here."

For what seemed like ages, they followed the skipping, hopping creatures with their tap-dancing voices through the closely grouped trees that gave off Jazzy sounds as random breezes lifted their leaves and occasional sunlight poured musical patterns about them.

'Days seem to last so long here,' thought Tristan. "Scherzo, I feel hungry."

Scherzo immediately delved into a pocket inside his multi-coloured coat and produced a small, clear bottle filled with light-mauve liquid.

"From this bottle sup, it's bound to fill you up!"

"Looks rather weird," Tristan said, losing his appetite. Scherzo insisted he drink it, however, so, giving it a brief inspection and finding no bad smell or otherwise, he took a sip. Like the liquid Prince Andante had given him, it tasted full of different fruits; though he found it hard to tell what sorts of fruits they were. The Jammings watched him, their smiling white mouths taking up half their fluffy faces. Tristan took another sip and handed it back to Scherzo whose hair turned the same colour as the liquid.

"Quite nice!" he admitted.

"Conn Ductor's home brew, is always good for you!" the cheerful little fellow exclaimed.

They continued on their way, with the Jammings obviously enjoying acting as guides; their chatter increasing as they cartwheeled, jumping stiffly head-over-heels and showing off as the displayed hand-stands. Soon, Tristan realised why they were so increasingly happy as Scherzo pointed said,

"Manchild, see and sing and laugh, over there lies the great Percussion Path!"

Not more than four hundred yards ahead of them was a clearing.

"I think it's getting darker," Tristan said. "So, thank goodness we know where we are!"

"Yes. You are right, we must stop for lapse of light," Scherzo agreed.

"Is it safe? What about the enemy?"

"If anything evil attempts to approach us, the Jammings will warm by making a fuss," Scherzo reassured.

Tristan was so tired he didn't argue. He rubbed his weary eyes, sat down, and watched Scherzo produce a silver handkerchief from his many-pocketed jacket, which, when unfolded, became a blanket; its edges embroidered with green and golden Quaver. Putting it over Tristan, Scherzo said, "Even in the raging, coldest storm, this will help you sleep and keep you warm!"

"Thank you!" he yawned, gratefully. As the Jammings and Scherzo did a little dance, he fell asleep....

.... and was back home in bed; everything normal. He was worried that he had not done his homework and what Mrs. Clayton would say. He saw the old boat keeper. He was trying to say something. He came closer and closer until his face was like a moon eclipsing the sun. It grew darker and darker. Then, there was a harsh sound. A huge black cat with one enormous green eye was scratching at his bedroom window, trying to get in. He attempted to cry out for his father; he couldn't make a sound! He couldn't move and the bedroom window was slowly opening and the huge black cat with the enormous green eye..... mauling..... scratching..... sleep thudded him with hard knuckles....

Tristan woke with a start. 'What an awful dream!' he thought. Scherzo smiled at him; he was talking to three Jammings. "Forget about your dream-fright, now is the time of new light." He handed Tristan the bottle of mauve liquid. Tristan took a mouthful and felt much better for it.

"Dixie, Be-Bop and Swing, will make travel an easy thing," Scherzo said and they followed the three Jammings who were soon joined by many more; their antics made the time pass quickly.

The Percussion Path was paved with brass coloured cobbles, having the appearance of Cymbals. It was about fifteen feet wide and stretched far into the distance.

The trees lined the path in regular, almost geometric fashion. Sometimes, large rocks that looked like big stone Harmonicas with holes where the mouthpiece should be, were arranged in groups. Scherzo told Tristan that these were jamming dwellings and that the main part of them was underground; these being merely the entrances and the exits. Sure enough, every so often, Tristan saw little light-beige fluffy heads with enormous smiling white mouths sticking out of the holes. Several of these dwellings, however, seemed to be damaged or shattered completely. When Tristan asked why this was this way, Scherzo told him that is was Discord spies that often did the damage when they were roaming Jazz doing mischief to anyone connected with Harmony. Tristan hated the Discords for this and rightly so for the Jammings were kind, harmless creatures.

They came to a clearing where the main Jamming dwellings were situated in one place. There, the companions were greeted by the two Chiefs of the Jammings; Ragers and Baysee Blues. For protection, Ragers gave Scherzo a treasured diamond dagger that they found long ago. Baysee Blues gave both companions a song of luck. A song that all the Jammings joined in to sing. Then, after friendlier, more entrancing exchanges, Scherzo and Tristan carried on with their Jamming guides.

Occasionally, along the way, the Jammings picked little white drum-shaped berries that grew on banjo bushes and ate them with a crunching tap-dancing relish.

Tristan found that the Forest of Syncopation was somewhat like a great long hall. The spaces that were high up, in between the trees' foliage, were like many windows in a roof and the path was straight. Tristan recalled that he had once read how the Romans built roads in Britain straight so that no enemy could hide round the band to ambush them. This road was like that. It gave one a sense of security. But, after another hour or so, in the distance he saw a bend in the road. Well, all roads had to bend somewhere after all and there was a small rock hill in the way.

They carried on... until - "Did you hear that?" Tristan asked, alarmed. He could tell by Scherzo's reaction that he had. Scherzo's hair turned magenta. They halted. The Jammings started to chatter nervously. The sound was that of jarring, careless noise.

"By the sound that is coming, I think they are Discords from Din," Scherzo said, hurriedly. "Manchild, we must go by the path's side, behind the trees we can hide."

The Jammings were already jumping up and down and scurrying off into the trees. Scherzo grabbed Tristan's hand and made a dash for the nearest cover but Tristan tripped with a loud 'OOOF' over a fallen trumpet branch. "Oh, great galloping gargoyles!" he moaned.

Two large and ominous figures came swaggering round the bend, just in time to see this happen. They were covered in heavy bluish-green metal - like armour, almost in the shape of wrinkled, bulging jackets and trousers; except the metal suits seemed to, and indeed were, parts of the discord. Like shells of turtles. They had ugly metal masks over their faces – one with a sneering mouth sticking out a horrid fleshy black tongue – the other squint-eyed and mealy-mouthed with a wobbling black tongue. From what Tristan could make out of their hands, they were dirty metal and hairy. They seemed to be all metal except for their extravagant fleshy tongues that they stuck out proudly to make disgusting noises with. Their whole appearance was grim and messy. 'So, these are Discords,' Tristan thought. 'Awful!'

"Lookee Jangle Luggs mate, two spittle-guts!" said one in a terrible voice.

"Yea. Let's smash their cads in," replied the other in a voice even more horrible. "Bambully boozle over bonas, eh, Jungle Mugg."

Both took out long, jagged metal sticks and started clanking and banging forwards; at the same time whirling the sticks in the air, making a frightful noise that made Tristan think his head was going to explode. He felt frightened and faint. Scherzo pulled him up and stood in front.

"Lay low behind the forest trees, let Scherzo take care of these!"

"But...look..." Tristan hesitated.

"Only I can fight this foe, you must go!" Scherzo stressed. Tristan gave one gaze ahead at the evil-looking couple crashing towards them and decided Scherzo was right. He sped into the nearest clump of trees.

Scherzo's hair radiated all colours of the rainbow. The nearer the frightful Discords thumped, the more his hair seemed to glow. The Discords were charging now, yelling and cutting the air with their weapons and producing an unbearable noise. Tristan covered his ears. Scherzo simply stood his ground.

Obviously surprised that Scherzo still seemed so unaffected by their clatter, the Discords halted. The taller and uglier of the pair, Jangle Luggs, made a heartbreaking thrust at Scherzo, but the little fellow quickly clapped his hands and let out a beautifully pure musical sound. Both the Discords' weapons shattered into a thousand dirty pieces. They covered their scaly holes, where ears should have been, and thumped up and down in agony; dazed and defeated. Quickly, Scherzo turned and ran to Tristan. He seemed somewhat exhausted.

"Come into the forest's depths, we must run - it's only just begun!"

Drawing heavy breaths, they hurried between the dense foliage until they could no longer hear the dreadful groans of the Discords on the Percussion Path. The Jammings were nowhere to be seen.

"How did you do that to the Discords?" Tristan asked at last.

"Conn Ductor so bright, gave me that power just right," was his reply. Tristan nodded, knowingly as they walked and walked and walked.

"We're lost!" Tristan said at last. "I'm sure we're going round in circles!"

Scherzo merely smiled and kept on.

The day was waning into lapse-light – the colours of the surroundings draining not so much into darkness, but as a water-colour picture where all the hues of paint run out leaving only black and white. They stopped and Tristan slumped to the ground. Scherzo unfolded the silver blanket and placed it over the boy.

"Goodnight!" Tristan said, rather unhappily, with a face as long as a week of rain.

Suddenly, there was a sound! Tristan rubbed his eyes. There was a movement! Dixie skipped out of the undergrowth, then Be-Bop from a nearby tree, then Swing appeared and, linking arms with his fellows, did a cheerful tap-dance!

"Now, Manchild, no need to complain, our friends are with us once again," Scherzo said.

"Yes. Oh, and do call me Tristan!" Tristan said with a tired smile and fell peacefully asleep.

*Whether it was just Tristan's over-active imagination or not,
the trees' branches gave the appearance of all manner
of brass instruments: trumpets, clarinets,
trombones, and saxophones.*

5

Across the Acoustic

"What are you talking to them about?" Tristan asked with a yawn as he woke his third day in Audia to see Scherzo with the three Jammings.

Scherzo handed Tristan the bottle of liquid. "With the Percussion Path no longer in view, I am asking the Jammings what next to do."

Tristan took a mouthful of mauve liquid and immediately felt wide awake. "Well, what did they suggest?"

Scherzo folded up the blanket and took back the bottle, for once taking a sip himself. "As far as I can see, this seems the way to me." He pointed South-Eastward. "We cannot follow the Percussion Path out, for there may be more Discords about."

"But the way you're pointing seems to be going deeper into the Forest!"

"There is but one way to see, I'll follow the Jammings and you follow me!"

"If you insist!" Tristan said, doubtfully, looking about him as they started walking once more. The Jammings chattered and danced as more of them joined the journey. To Tristan, it seemed as if they were just going absurdly deeper into the Forest of Syncopation instead of forwards and out as they were supposed to be.

"Look, Scherzo, are you sure this is the best way?" Tristan asked after a while.

Scherzo, his hair bright purple, just turned and smiled.

"Oh, well," Tristan sighed. "I don't know where I'm going but I'll be glad when I get there!"

Soon, they came to an area with fewer and fewer trees.

Then, suddenly, "Wait! There's a noise!" Tristan said. Hurriedly, they dashed behind the trees and the Jammings scurried under bushes. There was a thump, thump, thump of heavy, rough-shod feet pounding their way along. Soon, Tristan could make out a large, ugly figure scudding noisily towards them. It was a Discord, sporting a dirty, sickly, yellow-metal suit with a helmet-shaped like a jagged flame and a mask with squint-eyes and a dribbling mouth with long teeth and slimy tongue wagging about. "Must skedaddle. Must skedaddle," it was muttering to itself.

"Dreadful!" Tristan whispered, as the Discord banged passed them in a frightful hurry.

After a short while, the companions emerged.

"Why was he in such a disgusting rush?" Tristan asked.

"All Discords must be leaving their acts of sin, returning as fast as they can to Din. With the loss of their Interrupter power, they will be growing weaker by the hour." Scherzo replied. And, gathering their friends, the Jammings, the two companions carried on to the borders of Jazz.

When lapse-light came once more, they slept soundly with the Jammings all about them, chattering and eating white drum-berries.

In the morning, they set out once more. This was Tristan's fourth day in Audia. The Jammings were continuously dancing happily beside them. Their simple joy in life made Tristan feel a great warmth towards them. But, as the trees continued to thin more and more, the furry creatures fell off with chattering 'bye-byes' one by one; then in pairs, then in groups. Dixie, Be-Bop, and Swing were the last to depart as the open light began to flood through the sparse Jazz trees. They said 'Farewell!' and 'Good luck!' in their own very special tap-dancing way. Tristan was sad to see them go.

Before long, unhindered daylight was streaming in everywhere – the light was no longer tinted silver-green foliage or bronzed when reflected from each tree's bark. It was as if there was a series of tall open doors up ahead. They had reached the edge of Syncopation Forest.

"Oh, well, out of the frying pan!" Tristan muttered out loud. Scherzo scratched his magenta hair and nodded as they walked across the borders of Jazz together.

Before them and around them were fields covered by marvellous flowers with large, musical blooms. Scherzo told Tristan that these were the fields of Fioritura.

Tristan could barely make out a range of mountains in the distance. Scherzo told him these were the Amp Mountains of Pop.

Scherzo shared how they must go across the front field of Fioritura until they reach the large, flowing Acoustic River. Once they crossed the Acoustic River, they must then go through the rock plains of Roll before reaching the feet of the Amp Mountains.

"Seems such a long way still!" Tristan sighed.

"Then we must not talk or delay, we must start right away!" Scherzo said, taking out the bottle of liquid. Tristan was hoping that just once Scherzo would surprise him and produce a plate of bacon and eggs or spaghetti bolognaise, or even just a bar of chocolate from his many-pocketed jacket! Scherzo handed him the bottle of mauve liquid.

So, the two friends set out together on the next part of their journey through the Fields of Fioritura. Tristan remembered how he once thought, 'Who needs friends anyway.' Wouldn't the twins, Beatrice and Florence be proud of him - how he made such a wonderful friend in Scherzo! They would love to be here and share in these new memories too.

Tristan was in awe of all the amazing sights enveloping him. As they strolled along, he appreciated all the many flourishing and flowering magical blooms about and beyond and, of course, Scherzo as well, fitting in perfectly with the florid embellishment of melodic multi-colored blossoms that were stunning. Calming, ambient tunes wafted this way and that as the soft breeze flowed by them, but they seemed weakened from what they had once been as Scherzo stressed. Still, how lovely the soft tunes were. It gave Tristan a warm and comforting feeling to be with his jolly, rhyming friend. Like music, true friendship refreshes the soul.

Accompanying the blossoms' songs - Tristan's heard buzzing and humming in rhythm with the songs. Amongst the densely lush flowers were all manner of glittering insects; there were warbling wasps, baritone bees, whistling worms, beautiful ballad butterflies and a choir of sapphire blue cicadaes, pink polka-dotted crickets, and golden grasshoppers. They were all in sync together, all in perfect harmony.

They walked a long time. Tristan began to feel how he would like to stay here forever and he started drifting into a deep daydream; he imagined himself floating through a sea of swirling petals with soothing music lulling him to... Just then a gentle push forced him back from his reverie. Scherzo was smiling at him: "Manchild, no time now to daydream, the end is nearer than it may seem"

And so, as they said 'good-bye' to the fields of Fioritura, they came to the long, sloping, golden bank of the Acoustic River. They walked down and at the bottom, watched the musical flow of the widest river Tristan had ever seen. As it went on its fabulous course, it gave off all manner of chiming, whistling, and bubbling tunes.

"Goodness, me!" Tristan gazed, wide-eyed.

"Yes. The water here that so freely flows, is the life blood of musical Audia, wherever it goes," Scherzo said, his hair turning pea-green. "Many times it has been attacked by the evil one, but stopping it cannot be done!"

"Good!" Tristan scratched his head. "Look, I'm thirsty, Scherzo. Is it all right to drink the water of the Acoustic?" Scherzo gave a consenting nod and both of them drank from the river. Tristan found the water wonderfully cool and refreshing.

"Through Syncopation forest and Jazz we have gone, the fields of Fioritura we have crossed fast and strong, - so to cross the Acoustic is now really right, and then reach Pop by starting light," Scherzo said, seeing lapse-light approaching.

"But how?" Tristan asked. "There is no bridge as far as I can see, and we have no boat and it is certainly too far to swim!"

"No bridge has ever been built across, at the moment I'm at a complete loss," Scherzo admitted.

"Then, I think I can provide," said a curious, squeaky voice.

Both Scherzo and Tristan turned to see a short, thin creature with large, yellow eyes that were liquid and luminous. It was like a wizened man of indeterminate age, completely bald with a greeny-yellowish skin and a short, stumpy tail - reminding Tristan of some sort of cross between a man and a lizard.

"I think I can provide!" it repeated, stepping closer and rubbing its hands – his slimy skin glistening and his slimy tail slowing circling behind. He smelt of seaweed and rotten bananas.

"I see, and just who might you be?" Scherzo asked, suspiciously.

"I? Why I be Rubato," it squeaked. "This is Rubato's home!"

"Where?" Tristan asked, his nose twitching slightly as Rubato's odour nagged at his nostrils.

"Here!" it squeaked impatiently. "And Rubata CAN provide!"

"How?" Tristan didn't like this creature one iota.

47

"Ah-ha," Rubato squeaked teasingly. "Rubato has a tunnel that goes from the bank here," he pointed with a long, green, glistening finger displaying an inordinately long nail, "to the bank there." He pointed to the bank way over at the other end.

"I don't believe a word of it!" Tristan exclaimed. Saying nothing, Scherzo simply eyed the creature with careful, suspicious scrutiny.

"It's true, oh yesss, it's true; Rubato can! But first you must do a little something for I who provide!" He rubbed his long hands together in an extremely off-putting fashion.

"And what exactly is it that we must do?" asked Tristan, annoyed with this strange unwholesome creature.

"Ah-ha!" he cried, peering with jelly eyes at Scherzo. "Rubato has a bubbly spume and boggle-pots of a brother called Rubatee and he has stolen my pink wig. He is hiding from Rubato in river, just beneath the surface over there." He pointed to a nearby area of the Acoustic.

"What Robato wishes you to perform is to look over and talk to naughty Rubatee." He pointed to Scherzo. "So, that whilst he is distracted, Rubato the good can nab him and retrieve said wig of pink!"

"And if I am to trap him in this way, what would you suggest I say?" Scherzo asked with slight sarcasm, his hair turning caramel.

"Ask Rubatee if he is a naughty liar. If he says 'no' then you know that he is," replied the smirking creature.

"What if he says 'yes?'" Tristan asked, pointedly.

"Then he is lying!" Rubato cackled impatiently.

"And if I do this trick, you will take us under the Acoustic?" asked Scherzo, considering things.

"Look, Scherzo, don't listen to him. He doesn't mean it," Tristan urged. Truth is cool and soothing. Rubato's words were like acid. They were corrosive. They could dissolve truth in a heartbeat. Rubato reminded Tristan of rancid butter.

"Rubato shall provide!" squeaked Rubato with a loud hint of fierceness in his voice.

Scherzo looked at Tristan and shrugged his shoulders. "There appears to be no other way across, if we turn him down, we shall be again at a loss."

"This is perfectly absurd! I don't like it one little bit!" Tristan complained.

Rubato did a horrid little dance, wagging his tail and pointing to the spot where he said his brother was hiding. Scherzo walked over. Tristan began to follow.

"No. Rubato wants you to stay here," squeaked the slimy fellow, head tilting towards him in an off-putting way.

"Why?" retorted Tristan, defiantly.

"Because!" said Rubato, wagging a thin finger threateningly at the boy.

Tristan was about to argue when Rubato turned and hurriedly oozed over to Scherzo who, having reached the river-side, was peering down into the flowing water.

"Bend over some more, eh!" Rubato urged.

Scherzo did. He couldn't see anyone. Then, he thought he caught a glimpse of something down below. Someone that looked just like Rubato. He was about to relay this information when he realized that it was Rubato, or at least it was his reflection! The creature was standing right behind him. Scherzo felt a strong shove and, with a loud splash, he fell into the fast-flowing water!

There was a horrible squeaking laugh of triumph and Scherzo heard Tristan shouting for help.

Scherzo struggled with the moving water. Over his shoulder, he caught just a glimpse of Rubato disappearing down a covered hole with Tristan. Struggling as he sank beneath the bright melodic waters of the Acoustic, Scherzo began to drown.

*Amongst the densely lush flowers were all manner of glittering
insects; there were warbling wasps, baritone bees, boogying beetles.*

6

The Seeker

Dense darkness into black ink, swirling in solution gradually disappearing, getting thinner, clearer as the light crept back into Scherzo's eyes. He was lying on what must have been the river's bank. A man with a brown face and flock of warm red hair, flecked grey was kneeling over him. He had a kind smile on his face that stretched between two big red sideburns.

Scherzo felt his strength returning. "To whom do I owe thanks, for bringing me up on Acoustic's banks?" he gasped, his hair turning ocean blue, then violet.

"I am Sim Parth-Hee, the Seeker," the man said, helping Scherzo to his feet. "And right now, I seeketh to help thee."

"Then, without further ado, I sincerely thank you," Scherzo said, adding somewhat desperately, "Have you seen my friend, stranger? I have great fear he is in deadly danger!..."

....It was extremely uncomfortable lying slumped over the wicked creature's scaly shoulder in a steely grip. Every so often Tristan cried out as the two went deeper and deeper down the tunnel. But it was pointless. He did it more to complain than to fetch help. Soon, however, Tristan could see a light glowing at the end of the dark, dripping tunnel.

Rubato slimed into a big, round room hewn from the same hard rock and mud that the tunnel was created from. It was lit by rough, roundish stones covered with luminous lichen. There were many tunnels that led off in all directions from the room.

Suddenly, Rubato dropped Tristan onto the floor with a loud thump.

"Ouch!" snapped the boy. "Don't do that!"

Rubato chuckled.

"Slimy toad!" Tristan complained. He was about to add something more when, with a hiss and tail wagging, Rubato started a nasty thumping little dance in the middle of the floor; calling in a revolting voice, "Rubatee, Rubatum, come. Rubato has provided." Then, he quickly stopped dancing. From a corner in the room, he retrieved what must have been what he called his pink wig and proudly placed it on his head.

Tristan could hear noises in two of the other tunnels and, looking around, his eyes were suddenly transfixed in horror. In the corner were two piles. One was of gold, gems, swords, and armour. Tristan recognised one particular set of armour – a dirty, sickly yellow colour with a helmet shaped like a jagged flame and a squint-eyed mask with a dribbling mouth and long fangs. The only thing missing was one fleshy tongue. Yes, it was the hurrying Discord's metal but what happened to the occupant? No need to ask, for the other pile was of all types of …. bones! Tristan gazed at Rubato again and stared at his pink wig. Well, it was not a nice pink for the longer he looked at the wig, Tristan could tell that each strand of pink was a strand of dried flesh. Sickening!

Tristan listened to the sound of scurrying footsteps coming closer down the tunnels and was horrified as he realised, 'They're going to eat me!...'

…In the meantime, Scherzo related the kidnapping to Sim Parth-Hee. They both scoured the ground for Rubato's hidden entrance to the tunnel. The light was disappearing fast.

"Thou must feel the ground, for bodies of all living

things sendeth out vibrations," Sim Parth-Hee said. "Put thy palms to yon earth and feel."

Scherzo followed the stranger's instructions, but it just wasn't any good. Conn Ductor's power had been greatly used up and he needed to prevent what little he had left from fading. Time was running out – his hair turned murky brown and he began to despair.

Sim Parth-Hee, on hands and knees, looked a curious sight in his dusty old auburn robe and cloak with long, red boots worn on the outside of tucked-in trousers. Suddenly, he said, "Come thou hither worthy, yon ground be hollow beneath mine hands and, as stars against the sun, sendeth vibrations into my very being." He dug strong, brown fingers into the shaded golden turf and lifted up a hidden circular trap door...

...The three Rubats stood before Tristan, gnashing sharp teeth, licking wet lips, and menacingly wagging their short tails behind them. All were equally as horrible as each other. Rubato, still sporting his nasty wig, had greenish-yellow skin; the one called Rubartee was a grisly shade of greenish-red, and Rubatum was a slimy greenish-brown.

Tristan felt frightened. Then, he remembered Melody's gift. Whilst the three Rubats joined horrible, scaly hands and did an off-putting pre-dinner dance – in front of the dinner, namely Tristan – he slipped one hand into his right pocket and grabbed hold of Melody's gem. It seemed strangely warm and fear left him as he began to think rationally. All he had to do to escape was to switch on the golden tape and return home. So, as inconspicuously as possible, he attempted to pull his hidden recorder round from his side so he could turn the tape around. Gently, he moved his hand and managed to pull his machine nearer.

Suddenly, Rubato, who had been keeping one 'jelly' eye on him all the time, stopped his dance and, jumping forward, grabbed the tape player and pulled it off Tristan's shoulder.

"What's this item, eh?" he hissed in his slimy weasel voice, holding it up.

When Tristan refused to reply, Rubato examined the machine closely. He managed to turn it on but, since the tape hadn't been turned over, nothing happened.

"What does item provide? Answer!" squeaked Rubato impatiently. "Tell or I will gobble you up whole!"

The other Rubats rubbed their swollen purple-veined bellies.

"Yesss," Rubartum hissed. "Yessss. Let's put an end to him just a little bit now!" Rubata nastily suggested, his blue-tongue slipping round his lips like a flattened bullfrog flopping out of two soggy pieces of mouldy toast.

"Look, when your only tool is a hammer, all problems start looking like nails! Give it to me!" Tristan said, hurriedly. "I'll show you!"

"Oh, no. Oh, no. Tell Rubato!" Rubato cried angrily. "Not show. Tell I."

"If you get any crosser, you'll burst your face," Tristan snapped, defiantly. "Just hold the machine then. Whosoever holds it shall have....have one wish granted. You see, it's a wishing machine from Harmony. It only has one wish left."

"Eh!" cried Rubato, eyes all aglow with greed. "If what you say is truth, then by right, the last wish is Rubato's who provided!"

The other two Rubats glared at each other with jealousy gleaming in their eyes. "What of us?" they whined. But Rubato wasn't listening. He was already holding the machine firmly and opening his mealy-mouth to make a wish.

"Rubato wishes..." he began. But, before he could finish, his brothers jumped on him! They started fighting – kicking and scratching each other for possession of the recorder. Rubato dropped it as Rubatum's dirty teeth sank into his scaly hand and Rubatee angrily pulled his pink wig apart.

Springing to his feet, Tristan grabbed his machine and

ran as fast as he could down the nearest tunnel.

It wasn't long before Rubato realised that Tristan had tricked him. He let out a frightful scream of rage.

It couldn't have been more than five minutes later when Scherzo and Sim Parth-Hee, hearing the scream, reached the Rubat's circular room. No one was there!

"We are too late, the Manchild has met some horrible fate," gasped Scherzo, staring mournfully at the pile of bones in the corner.

"Thou are wrong, worthy," Sim Parth-Hee said. "Full four vibrations do I feel. Three art soiled, yet one is pure. Thy young friend liveth!" He raised sensitive palms outwards and, in a circular motion, rotated them in front of one tunnel after another. Suddenly, he stopped. "This one yonder," he said, pointing to a tunnel just to his right.

Tristan could hear the frightful three gaining on him in the dripping darkness of the tunnel. He could hear the angry gnashing of teeth, the slimy gurgles, and hissing. 'If they catch me now,' he thought, 'they're bound to eat me before I get a word in edgeways.'

He fumbled with his recorder as he ran, attempting to take out the tape. At last, he managed it but, in his nervous haste, he dropped it. As he hurriedly stooped to retrieve the golden object, something heavy, stinking, and sticky jumped on his back.

"Yesss. Now Rubato's got you."

In a frenzy, Tristan took out Melody's gem, giving Rubato a cracking backward blow on the head with it. "Owww. I hurt!" squealed the scaly creature in pain, falling off a relieved Tristan and onto the ground, sobbing.

Tristan turned to run but Rubatee and Rubatum rushed at him. Rubatee held him around the legs whilst Rubatum tried to pry the gem from Tristan's desperate grip. Robatum received a thud on the chest for his trouble and started yelping. Rubatee bit into Tristan's leg. With a cry of pain,

Tristan dropped the ball! All three Rubats were now on top of him, about to sink sharp yellow fangs into his body when,

All three Rubats were now on top of Tristan.

"Halt thy wicked deed!" Sim Parth-Hee stood before them.

Scherzo, diamond dagger twinkling in hand, didn't waste words, he thrust it at the treacherous Rubatee, giving him a terrible wound in his stomach; from which thick dark purple liquid gushed out. Immediately, the others stopped and jumped to their feet. Scherzo was about to strike again, but Sim Parth-Hee stayed his hand.

"Alright, alright. We provide," hissed the weasel-mouthed Rubato.

Scherzo rushed to where Tristan lay. "Please, Manchild, your good friend tell, are you ill or are you well?"

"Ooh!" Tristan rubbed his head. "I think I'm alright. Except for this," he nodded to the place where Rubatee had bitten him. It was bleeding badly.

Sim Parth-Hee turned a knowing gaze on the two cowering Rubats. "Thou hast done much evil," he said.

"Don't kill I, don't, don't!" squealed Rubatum.

"Shut it!" hissed Rubato, threateningly.

"Thou must promise to give up thy carrion acts of murder and show the way to yonder side of the flowing Acoustic!" The Seeker was stern.

"What if Rubato do? What will you provide?"

"Thy lives and the life of thy stricken brother!"

Scherzo looked at the fallen Rubatee. "You will have to promise something else instead, this carrion creature is almost dead." His hair turned silver.

"My promise remaineth," Sim Parth-Hee assured. "What is thy answer?"

Rubato cast a baleful look around. He couldn't escape. "Alright," he hissed resentfully.

Sim Parth-Hee stepped forward and, kneeling, placed his left hand on the dying Rubat's stomach, still oozing steaming liquid. Immediately, Rubatee's eyes opened and before the astonished gaze of the others, the wound healed itself.

"Where life remaineth, I can mend," the Seeker said, solemnly.

Rubatee rose, slowly checking the place where his wound had been; making sure its healing hadn't been some sort of trick.

Next, Sim Parth-Hee laid his palm on Tristan's wound which also healed itself.

"How do you do this?" Tristan asked, amazed.

"I have been seeking for so long that I have discovered many, many things."

So saying, the Seeker gazed at Rubato who had to keep his part of the bargain now and this he did with all the bad will in the world.

The companions followed the sulking Rubats back down the tunnel and into the large, foul-smelling room. Then, they followed the slinking three down another tunnel...until, "Here!" hissed Rubato bitterly, pushing up a circular trapdoor above his head.

Outside, it was still lapse-light. They all climbed out. Sure enough, they were on the other side of the Acoustic. It was a great relief for Tristan to be able to breathe clean air once more.

"This is well done!" exclaimed Sim Parth-Hee. "Now, thine other promise remember."

But the Rubats had already jumped back into their tunnel and closed the moss-covered door with an angry 'thud!' Once back in their home, the Rubats tails thrashed angrily at the empty air and Rubato gave Rubatum and Rubatee each a nasty clout. Then, an especially hard one for Rubatee who had wrecked his wig. Then, they all sped back down the tunnel; gnashing teeth and thinking of what more mischief they could do.

As they ran, "Yes, I know HE will be most interested in my item of information!" Rubato chuckled and wagged his slimy tail.

"If I never see them again it will be too soon!" Tristan said.

"If your watch on a Rubat is ever slack, you will wake up with its promise sticking in your back," Scherzo said. Then, as his hair glistened turquoise, he turned and added,

"Seeker, called Sim Parth-Hee, will you join our company?"

Sim Parth-Hee smiled sadly. "Only until the demise of lapse-light, when shadows flee and dangers lurk not hidden," he answered. "I know of thy task, worthy, yet I also have mine. We all seeketh for something. In the end, it is tiring, yet then, it is only the beginning. I seeketh for that which will make me seek no more."

They all sat down. Scherzo placed a blanket over Tristan and Sim Parth-Hee told them this story:

"At the Northernmost corner of Audia, an uncharted land lies. A land without a name or with a name that was lost long ago. In that land stands a large cave in which a singing stone singeth of a time stolen forever. On this stone, two tiny pools in carven holes flow without ceasing. These two pools be the eyes of a witch's daughter, crying endlessly for lost love. Oh, cruel fate of her beauty, she was sucked into the centre of that enchanted stone because of a spell woven by her jealous mother, Marr Levelent, to preventeth her betrothal to a man she loved. This was long ages past. The man whom she loved pledged his troth to her for all-time but had not the skill to release her. Thus, for ages beyond memory, this man searcheth, like a shadow in the sun, the many lands of Audia; seeking the knowledge of the skill to free her."

"Are you that man?" asked Tristan, but he needed no answer.

When lapse-light ceased, Sim Parth-Hee bade them farewell and went on his lonely way to seek and seek and perhaps one day to find. But that, as they say, is another story.

*When lapse-light ceased, Sim Parth-Hee bade them farewell
and went on his lonely way to seek and seek
and perhaps one day to find.
But that, as they say, is another story.*

7

A Melancholy Dance

The gleaming bronze-coloured bank of the Acoustic River continued its course for some time until, after the companions stopped for refreshment from their near empty bottle, the soft land became rougher ground. So, it was on Tristan's fifth day in Audia that he and Scherzo entered Roll.

"Hard going, isn't it!" Tristan said, climbing over stones that were increasingly becoming rocks and boulders.

They were soon climbing much more steeply as the Roll rocks merged into the foot of the Amp Mountains. If Tristan got stuck, Scherzo, his hair changing colour, would pull him up. They were both climbing with their eyes down to judge the lay of the Mountain's roughness. So, you can imagine Tristan's shock when, instead of jagged rocks like radio-waves carved out of stone, he came upon a pair of large, green, pointed boots. He reached out and grabbed Scherzo to stop himself from losing his balance.

They both looked up.

A tall man towered above them, cloaked in livid green garments and hood with only his face showing. It was a face that hardly seemed real – so green, so ugly, so wax-like, and …. it had no eyes. Instead, above his right shoulder, there hovered a luminous green eye; its ball was the size of a curled-up child and it twinkled maliciously. The man's cloak

61

billowed like vultures' wings all set for some wicked flight.

"Ha!" the Green man cackled. "So, the little Slinker was right, you're no Concord."

"Little Slinker?" Tristan gazed anxiously at Scherzo.

"I am afraid that the evil Rubato who made so much fuss, has slimed from his hole and betrayed us," Scherzo sighed, his hair turning viridian. "The danger has come fully into view, for the evil one now knows of you."

"Yes. My Master will be most pleased," the creature carped. "He has been busy seeking what your wicked Master stole. I was also sent to search. But, the eye, Obi Aleatoree, has found another thing of equal importance. Ha! Ha! Yes!"

"You may as well return to Cacophony, you won't get the better of me," said Scherzo, his hair turning many colours. As quickly as a frog on a hot plate, he jumped at the Green man with his diamond dagger whistling musically in the still air.

The Green man leapt back, his hovering eye shining brightly as a beam shot from its dark green pupil. The rocky slope that Tristan and Scherzo were on turned to slippery glass. Both tumbled helplessly down it, landing with a dull thud on a ledge ten feet below. Apart from bruises, they were miraculously unhurt.

"You shall never finish your task now. It's known, fool!" cackled the Green man, pointing at Scherzo. "I shall keep you here 'till my Master has completed his search. Then, he shall put an end to you with the rest of the cursed Concords!" And, pointing at Tristan, he said, "You – he may have other plans for!"

With that, a loud breeze whisked up like crackling electric static.

Scherzo's hair flickered rainbow colours as he fingered his diamond dagger in extreme agitation. "With the Eye, you are clever, alone, you couldn't defeat me ever," he answered.

Suddenly, there was a loud sizzling, as of something

being switched on and a torrent of football-sized hailstones rained down upon the two companions. They both cowered, covering their heads with their arms, as fissures opened in the rocks; flames shooting up formed a circle around them. The Green one hissed and danced. Well and truly trapped, Tristan felt his head fill with horrible moaning, crackling noises.

Scherzo stood up and tried to get through, but with the hailstones and flames, it was impossible.

"What are we going to do, Scherzo?" Tristan cried out desperately.

The flames were rapidly closing in on them. Although the hailstones continued to fall, they did not hit Tristan and Scherzo. For some reason, the Green man wanted to keep them alive.

Mustering all of his strength, Scherzo took painful, squint-eyed aim and threw his diamond dagger at the shimmering servant of the wicked Cacophony. The diamond blade missed, its whistling journey drowned in the increasing noise. The Green one laughed mockingly. But, as something that is aimed at a goal and misses may carry on to the good, so the dagger thumped with a musical 'clang' against a rock above the hovering Eye.

The rock dislodged and fell with a 'thud' on top of the Eye. Immediately, the flames and hailstones vanished as if they had never existed and the Eye closed, dulling as it floated to the floor. The Green man disappeared completely!

"We must hurry past and away; it would be folly to delay!" Scherzo commanded anxiously, his hair turning burnt sienna. He grabbed Tristan's hand and pulled him upright. They clambered hurriedly past the inanimate Eye. The diamond dagger was lost beneath a rock. Up and up they climbed until, through a gap in the rocks, they came upon a narrow road that wound away high into the heart of Pop. Scherzo told Tristan that this was the Beat Way.

The day was greying, soon it was lapse-light once more;

when shadows became secret hidden things. Tristan now simply couldn't shake off his increasing feelings of unease.

"Scherzo, it's getting quite dark. When are we going to stop and rest? I'm tired and hungry."

"Not long, keep humming your inward song," Scherzo replied, his hair turning blueberry blue.

'Not long,' felt like 'far too long!' The Beat Way didn't have a drop on one side anymore but ran between high walls of stone and it was like walking through a high, roofless tunnel. Tristan kept making pleading faces to stress the fact that he was tired but Scherzo was in one of his 'keep-on' moods.

Turning a corner, Tristan was fingering Melody's gem to see if it would prevent him from getting tired. Suddenly, it slipped from his hand and rolled into a thicket of prickly bushes that had leaves shaped remarkably like the machine-heads of guitars. Tristan ran after it and, pushing aside some of the branches, noticed an opening into a cave.

"Hey! Scherzo!" called the boy to the little fellow with tawny-coloured hair, "there's a cave behind these bushes! Might not be a bad idea to sleep in here. We'd be well and truly hidden." Tristan picked up the gem as Scherzo came over.

They pushed aside the bunched branches of the bush and crept in. It was really quite dark but it was dry and felt safe enough. They couldn't see very far, but the cave seemed fairly small. They decided that it was the best place to spend lapse-light. Sitting down, they made ready to sleep.

"I haven't eaten for ages," Tristan said, hungrily.

"My, at this hour, I wish I had your willpower!" Scherzo laughed softly as he handed the bottle to the boy. "Only a tiny drop, that is all we've got!"

"Don't you want any, Scherzo?"

Scherzo simply yawned and lay back, so Tristan finished it. Though it seemed to fill him, that night he dreamed of sandwiches thicker than haystacks with solid breeze blocks of butter, tomato, and cucumbers followed by cheeseburgers as big as the Wembley stadium crowded with many onions as football fans jammed together for a cup final. He was drinking hot chocolate from a storage tank when he woke to his sixth day in Audia.

Scherzo was still asleep. After folding up one blanket, Tristan stretched himself, rose to his feet and looked around. The cave was larger than he had thought. Inset to his left, he saw an opening. He walked over to it and poked his head cautiously through into what turned out to be a round room. Gazing in, he saw a beam of light shining down from the rock ceiling onto a circular wall made from bluish stone. Tristan gazed round for any other opening in the room. Seeing none, he concluded that the room was empty and therefore safe.

When he reached the blue wall, he found that it was in fact a wall. The light that fell from the ceiling made the silver water sparkly and luminously clear. As Tristan craned his neck to peer down, he thought he saw a form frail as a flower doomed to drop and die before the setting sun. It was dancing in merging light and water.

Tristan didn't know why but suddenly, he felt a feeling of great sorrow. A lonesome tear slid down his cheek and soundlessly dropped into the luminated water below. He was about to touch the water's curious surface with an outstretched finger when he heard a rasping electric noise, like a whirring static jar in the cave.

As he ran back to the entrance where Scherzo had been sleeping, he heard a wicked voice crackle, "Ah-ha!" Then, in a mixture of anger and triumph, "You couldn't escape the Eye of Obi Aleatoree!"

The wicked Green one had trapped Scherzo in a cage of zig-zagging electric bars that sizzled horribly. The large, hovering Eye's beam scanned all round the cave searching for Tristan. He stepped quickly back into the shadow of the entrance, not knowing what to do next.

"You may have chosen well where to hide," goaded the Green devil. "But, the Eye Aleatoree plucked from Obi, magic lord of Chaos, will always seek you out!"

The Green one's crackling voice flooded Tristan with trembling fear. He started backing blindly away from the entrance as the evil eye's beam cut through the cave, honing in on him.

Just as its malicious force grabbed him and he saw a sizzling cage form about him; just as he reached for Melody's gem; just as he thought it useless to struggle further, the back of his legs struck the low blue rock wall and he tumbled and fell backward into the well with a shimmering splash.

Immediately, all traces of capture disappeared. Tristan clutched onto Melody's gem. Trying to swim, he only floated further down and down and down; pulled into the depths by some unseen force. The clear sparkling water above him turned turquoise, then azure, then dark blue as we went deeper and deeper. Then, the dark blue surrounding him began to swirl and the water bubbled all manner of luminescent colours. It was as if he was in a whirlpool.

'Well, if I was going to drown,' he surmised, 'I would surely have drowned by now!'

The bubbles of clear colour began to shine and reflect like a million tiny mirrors, just like the bubbles his father insisted on overloading the Christmas tree with. Tristan was beginning to wonder if he would ever cease falling when suddenly and gently, he came to a halt. His eyes were bright with wonder as a soft silvery-blue light wrapped his vision. He blinked but the light still covered and filled his sight. He blinked again but it persisted. It was as if a living thing penetrated his vision and mind. Then, he realised that the place he found himself in was made of this nearly tangible light and he was completely dry! It was like being in the midst of and part of a fluffy cloud. For a while, he felt as dizzy as he had one Sunday lunchtime when his parents had invited the Cattons round for morning drinks and he'd secretly finished off the remainder of each sherry glass.

Then, before him emerged a beautiful woman, seemingly created from a more solid form of the very same light that surrounded him. Masses of pale blue hair flowed from her lovely head to the ground, sparkling like the bubbling water through which he had come.

"Welcome, child of tears!" she said in a wonderful voice, sounding like the cadence of a thousand flowing streams.

"Thank you. But, who are you?" Tristan ventured, gazing at her swirling radiance.

"I am Vina. I was once a magician's daughter from a land called Elsanador – a land filled with magnificent rivers that sang as we rowed; we saw diamonds sparkle on the beds of the light red water. Everything was brightly coloured and all Elsanadonians used boats to travel from place to place. These boats talked to their owners, other owners, and each other. These boats lived, for their wood came from the mystical forest of Withyheim. I am known, or was known, to one in your world, the Keeper who watches. I was the magician's daughter but a spell took me from Elsanador and brought me here to be a spirit of dancing atmosphere and of the well you tumbled through."

She was silent for a moment, then continued. "Thus, now I am Vina the Deathless Dancer," she said softly, seeming to come closer although Tristan didn't perceive any movement. "I am Vina, one who dances like a whisp through time and eternity like a whisper in the wind. Perhaps one day the Keeper of your world who watches will find a way to release me, but for now, having cared for your world, I say that the sun owes a favor of light to the moon; not abandoning it to darkness. So, I owe you a favor."

"A favour!" exclaimed Tristan. "Why?"

"Because you shed a tear for my dance when you gazed

into my heart. You shed a tear for my sorrow." She smiled. "And for a moment, you stilled the spell."

"I did?"

"Oh, yes, Tear child. Your tear reached my heart selflessly and stopped my melancholy dance for a brief spell. You gave me the form you see before you now. Without your precious little drop of liquid, I would have remained formless and dancing light and water as you see about you."

"I really don't understand!" Tristan was perplexed.

"There are many forms of existence that are beyond you. Without such as I, such as you could not be as you are. There are reasons for all things, though many must needs be hidden. It is good that the different ones meet from time to time. As long as such as you can feel for such as I, then there is hope left for both of us." She paused as the myriad shimmering hues of her swirling blue substance danced everywhere about her. "My dance is fearless; it is free; it does not fear any challenge. It is beneath no one, superior to no one, and full of magic, mystery, and enchantment. But, it is also a prison; a trap of the spell. It is now entirely me. Do you see?"

"I think I see," Tristan mused, not really seeing but perhaps half-way there; understanding that there was something that he could not touch, eat, or see that meant a great deal to him – music.

"Tell me what you desire and I shall help," she said softly.

Tristan told Vina about Obi Aleatoree and the floating Eye.

"Obi Aleatoree is the Eye Cacophony, lord of Chaos, uses. The disguise tells more than the man," Vina said. "At present, Cacophony is elsewhere. He is not the wry-mouthed Green one that is a form conjured up by the Eye to frighten you. Obi Aleatoree is the name of the Eye itself. Without Cacophony, its only power is illusion. Its illusions, however, are so strong that few can resist them and thus they can drive one mad or even destroy one completely. When you return, bathe your face in my water and do the same for your friend. I'll wash away the illusions. Then, to drive the evil Eye out, merely say, 'Cacophony' aloud and I shall help compel it to return to its Master."

"But..." Tristan began, wanting more explanation about this.

"I thank you, Tear child," Vina interrupted, suddenly seeming to drift further and further away from him. "Perhaps one day we shall come together again." Her words were like a memory.

The next thing Tristan knew was that he was in the bubbling, swirling liquid once more and, before he had time to think, he was sucked upwards. At first fast, then faster, then fastest. The bubbles disappeared. The water became dark blue, then azure, then turquoise, then light blue, and then he began to slow down amidst silvery-clear liquid. Slow, slower, slowest as a beam of light began to pull him up from the water.. and...

...Tristan stood completely dry beside the well. The sound of hissing electricity flooded every nook and cranny of the cave.

Through the opening, he could see Scherzo, still trapped in the cage of jagged electric-green bars. The Green man of Obi Aleatoree was talking angrily to him; asking questions and enraged that he received no answers. The little Concord was adamant in his silence. Then, suddenly, to Tristan's horror, the wicked Eye floated menacingly into his room.

"Oh, no!" Tristan gulped.

The Eye began glowing, seemingly as though a tornado was racing towards Tristan. Rocks started falling all around and hitting him as his legs became roots chaining him to the ground.

"It's an illusion! An illusion!" Tristan kept repeating to himself out loud and one of his hands grasped Melody's gem.

"You cannot defeat me, fool!" Obi Aleatoree cackled triumphantly as a sizzling cage formed around Tristan but a voice inside the boy, soft and calm kept repeating, 'An illusion. It's all just an illusion!'

Tristan turned and, although it almost drove him mad with pain, he went through the bars and lent over the wall. Instead of water, it was filled with giant yellow-fanged rats and long slimy snakes and huge spiders with long hairy legs all in a horrible stinking ooze of fluid.

"I must wash my face!" And, tears pouring down his skin, sweat pouring down his body, Tristan scooped the rats and snakes that bit and gnawed at his flesh and stung him excruciatingly. He could hardly bear or contain the pain. Feeling violently sick, he thrust his head into the seething mass. Instead of biting and stinging, he felt a cool, calming liquid cover his face. He felt fresh, alive, totally unhurt. All the rats and snakes and spiders had vanished.

He turned, staring at the evil hovering Eye that was now glowing more brightly and menacingly than ever. The Green man vanished.

"How can this be?" the Eye sizzled. "My power has no effect on you."

"And it never shall again!" Tristan said defiantly.

"Ha! But I still have the Concord captive!" the Eye crackled. "I shall destroy him!" With that, it sped over to make good its threat. It glowed in front of Scherzo, who screamed terribly. Who knows what frightful things he saw? Tristan hurriedly scooped another handful of water and, fearing any loss of time, ran over and threw it at Scherzo, wetting his neck and head completely. Immediately, Scherzo blinked, looking absolutely confused; as if he had been retrieved from some long and terrible nightmare.

The Eye glowed so much that it looked as if it would catch fire. "My Master shall know of this!" It screamed, shooting sparks of static electricity everywhere. Then, it grew brighter still. Tristan feared that it had more evil to play and so, at the top of his voice, "Cacophony!" he cried.

Immediately, the Eye blazed and streaming crackling fire, with a piercing scream, shot comet-like into the sky and out of sight.

"Scherzo," Tristan called anxiously, "are you alright?"

"Yes. Do not worry about me, but please tell how you managed to set us free."

Tristan took Scherzo over the wall and told him what happened. Scherzo listened more intently than he ever had to the boy before, marvelling at the story.

Then, after a wondering pause, Scherzo said, "Although it is truly mysterious what you say, we must linger here no longer, we must be away."

"Yes. Alright!" Tristan agreed, turning his gaze from the water where, far below, the spell returned as strong as ever and Vina vanished into her melancholy dance once more.

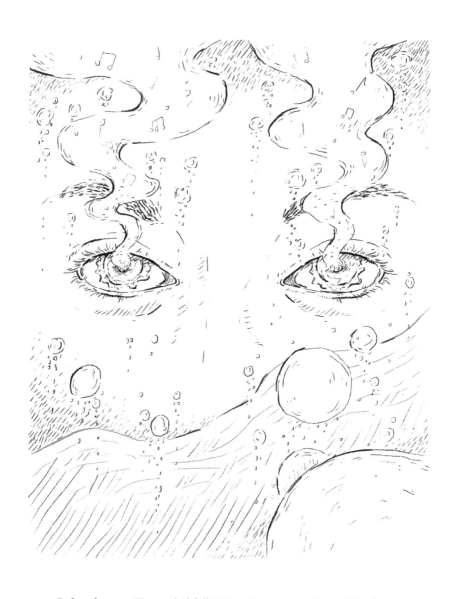

I thank you, Tear child," Vina interrupted, suddenly
seeming to drift further and further away from him.
"Perhaps one day we shall come together again."
Her words were like a memory.

Chapter 8

The Ring of Moog

Tristan glanced at Scherzo. The little fellow appeared to be growing rather weary. His hair, though still changing colour, was doing so with much less enthusiasm. Time was not on their side.

The Beat Way was becoming increasingly more level, as on all sides the Amp Mountains rose up to shoulder an electric-blue sky. Soon, they would be in the heart of Pop.

As they walked on, Tristan could see a plateau in the distance. In the middle of the plateau, a tall tower shaped remarkably like a Guitar rose into the sky. It was formed from craggy bluish rock and was surrounded by a huge fortified wall of reddish hue.

"The Mod tower of Bop Shoowah, there, all distance is unfurled, and from it we shall gaze into your world!" Scherzo's voice was uncommonly quiet.

"At last!" Tristan smiled at the curious landmark. "Almost there!"

The Beat Way climbed until it was level to the Plateau of Pop. They followed it until they came to the high red wall that served to protect Mod from intruders. A pair of large silver gates shaped like two enormous drums was in the wall, but they were tightly closed. On the gates were numerous black and golden stars and both half and full white moons. In the middle was a huge golden knocker in the shape of a guitar.

Tristan stood silently, considering for a moment.

"How are we going to get in?" he asked. "We can't push these massive gates open and the knocker is too high for either of us to reach."

"By ourselves we are small, but climb on my shoulders and we shall be tall!" Scherzo said, his hair turning damask red – and Tristan did.

There was no knock, however, but there were three long bursts of a thunderous electric Organ and, "Well, who is it?' a loud voice demanded. Tristan jumped down.

"We come from sweet Harmony, and Bop Shoowah we must see," replied Scherzo.

"Concords, eh!" the voice exclaimed.

"Look, please," Tristan urged. "Let us in. We've come so far to see Bop Shoowah and ask..."

"Never be ashamed to ask what you don't know!" the voice interrupted rather pompously. "But, never forget of your unspoken word you are master – your spoken word is master of you!"

The great gates opened into a large courtyard. The Tower of Mod, the sanctuary of Bop Shoowah, was in the middle, and rose up splendidly high. The two companions entered the courtyard.

"Good grief!" Tristan gasped, stopping in amazement. As he turned, he saw two giants towering by the gates; both almost fifteen feet high and immensely broad. Without a sound, they closed the gates.

Tristan was speechless as he looked at Scherzo, whose hair turned indigo in reply. The two giants were very hairy and their skin gleamed like mackerel scales. But, their faces, each with a large pendulous nose, were friendly. They wore one-piece leather garments like tunic-kilts – one dark blue, the other red - and each with a symbol of a silver guitar on a thick leather belt.

"Ah, don't worry about Bunkum and Bosh," said a figure striding energetically towards them.

"If I am not mistaken you are, the Honorable Bop Shoowah," Scherzo said, his hair slowly turning corn-flower blue.

"All creatures have a name. This is mine. Know as you are known, I always say," the figure replied.

'And what a curious figure!' Tristan thought. He was a tall, gaunt man whose head was bubbling with long, thick, curly hair – one half of which was silver and the other golden. On either side of his head was a long pointed ear that was barely visible. He had a kind, smiling face of indeterminate age, like a favorite remembered song. He wore a three-piece suit of gold embroidered with silver and black designs of stars and moons similar to those on the gates. A white guitar symbol was stitched boldly on the chest of his jacket. A silver cape billowed behind him as he walked and a dog-like creature with short, hairy legs sticking out from a tortoise-shell that covered his body trotted by his side.

"Heel, Yeah Yeah," said Bop Shoowah, halting merrily in front of the two. "Bunkum and Bosh are quite harmless, my friends – as long as you are my friends!"

"We are!" Tristan stressed, staring at Yeah Yeah, who was in the process of licking one of his fat front paws with his long purple tongue. "I'm Tristan," Tristan added. "How do you do?"

"Well enough!" exclaimed Bop Shoowah, rubbing his pointed chin in a pondering fashion. "I think I know something of what is happening outside Pop. Come this way if you will." He turned and they followed; Yeah Yeah bouncing along by their sides.

"However," Bop Shoowah continued, "I never like to think too much – thinking is like eating – if you eat just enough food, it carries you. If you eat too much, you must carry it!" He looked round at them, smiling. "Yes. That is it to a tee," he concluded.

"What is he saying?" Tristan whispered. "Has he got bats in his belfry or something?"

Scherzo shrugged his shoulders.

The three, along with Yeah Yeah, entered Mod through a door of the same design as the gates. They came into a large hall made bright by a blazing fire that danced merrily in a drum-shaped grate. Around the grate were six black chairs with golden half-moon backs. They looked very inviting indeed to the tired travellers.

"Come, sit down!" invited Bop Shoowah.

"Time is short, we mustn't delay, the Metronome must be sought today," Scherzo said, even though he, like Tristan, would have rather liked to rest.

"So be it!" said Bop Shoowah. "Tell me your story as quickly as you desire and your request."

So, Scherzo related the adventures of their journey and their peril and purpose to Bop Shoowah.

"I knew the Sound Reaper was abroad again," Bop Shoowah said, shaking his head. "If only the Waltz Lords were still about...if only my Lady Electrika had not... not..." he suddenly seemed very sad. Then, rubbing his forehead, "Danger is too important a thing to talk about seriously." He passed the mood away. "So you are a Manchild?' he asked, gazing at Tristan. "Well, well, it is most edifying to meet one."

"Thank you!"

"If we can get the Golden Metronome back, then we can prevent the evil one's attack," Scherzo interrupted to prevent any side-tracking.

Bop Shoowah looked straight at the little Concord. "Come with me, my friends," he said.

The two companions followed the Keeper of Pop to the foot of a large winding staircase. Again, the stair reminded Tristan of the keys of a piano.

"Well, it's up here. Follow me!" Bop Shoowah said, starting to climb. The two followed. Tristan was amazed at Yeah Yeah. Instead of the little creature running up after them, out popped scaly wings from under his shell and he started to fly with a loud bumble-bee buzz above them; sometimes upside down and sometimes right side up.

As they climbed, Tristan could see Scherzo growing considerably more tired. His hair was not changing colour but rather, he was losing it to the surrounding air.

"Yes. My Moog ring is here," began Bop Shoowah, contemplatively, "I hope you will be able to operate it as my Lady Electrika intended. I never mastered the knack myself. It was all rather beyond me. Besides, I am not interested in Lumio really. There's less to it than meets the eye."

"I'm sure I'll be able to manage it," Tristan assured.

"Yes," replied Bop Shoowah. "A key is of itself useless but if it can be made to turn a lock and open doors, then, and only then mind you, it becomes an article of value."

"I'm sure you're right." Tristan gave him a concerned look.

As they mounted the stairway even higher, Tristan could see the top of Amp Mountains through clear crystal windows. They were crimson and purple coloured with sunset. Yeah Yeah, with a quick lick of Bop Shoowah's face, disappeared round a bend in the twisting stair column.

"Almost there!" shouted Bop Shoowah. "Like a little something? A tasty Motown Nut for trendy people?"

He offered Tristan one from a silver pouch. Tristan declined. Bop Shoowah smiled and started cracking the nuts with his teeth. As they rounded the last bend, Tristan found himself in a small hall where two doors led off the hall.

"This one!" exclaimed Bop Shoowah, pointing to a door with a keyboard chiseled above the lintel and, continued, "You know, I haven't really had anyone to talk to for a long while except Bunkum and Bosh. Still, I prefer doing all the talking; saves time and prevents arguments."

After climbing all the steps, Tristan could see that they were very high up indeed. Yeah Yeah, landing with a 'yeah, yeah,' scurried into the room.

"Yes. I have been quite alone," Bop Shoowah carried on. "My last regular visitor was the Waltz Lord, Comm Poser, before he vanished. Funny, but there was something queer about him the last time he visited me. He was searching for something; never got it though, not here anyway. The next thing I knew, Cacophony came and destroyed my Garden of Pop and all my tune trees in revenge. He said it was for failing him. Never could figure the connection! Anyway, that was ages and ages ago before the evil one's imprisonment. Since my Lady Electrika... well, since then, the Moog ring has remained unused and everyone seems to have lost interest in Pop." He sighed as they entered a medium-sized room that was bare except for a lovely centerpiece that was a large circular keyboard. Scherzo propped himself against the wall. He knew what Cacophony was looking for but thought it best not to say so.

"Well, here it is!" Bop Shoowah said, going over the circular keyboard that was hovering in mid-air. "Manchild, come closer!" he urged. Tristan did.

"Step into the center," Bop Shoowah instructed. Immediately, the ring lowered to the height of Tristan's waist and, with the boy in the middle, left him about a foot of space inside the whole circumference.

"My! That's very good indeed. It accepts you!" exclaimed Bop Shoowah.

"How do I work this?" Tristan asked.

"Ah! Now, if my memory serves me well, I think you simply press one key after the other until something happens." Bop Shoowah sounded rather vague.

"Like this?" Tristan asked, pressing the nearest key. A deep distant note came from the circular keyboard. He pressed another key and another and another until all the notes emitted were high pitched and close. It was almost as if the sound was in Tristan's head. Then, a balloon-like object, about the size of a small coffee table top, appeared in front of Tristan.

"Well, I'll be a Rock's Grandmother. You've done it!" Bop Shoowah said enthusiastically.

Scherzo stepped closer, urging Tristan, "Tell it to search your home, to find our Golden Metronome."

"O.K.!" Tristan concentrated. "Please show me where Harmony's Golden Metronome is."

At once, a familiar scene appeared in the balloon. Not only did it show Tristan's world, but his country and his county. In fact, it showed the very town and street that he knew very well indeed!

"That's old 'Moley' Lampeter's house!" exclaimed Tristan, greatly surprised. "It's enough to make a cat laugh – under my nose all the time!"

And indeed, the Moog showed Mr. Lampeter's attic and, in a very dusty corner hidden beneath some storage boxes, "The Golden Metronome I see, oh what a joy to me," cried Scherzo, pleased.

The balloon suddenly vanished and the Moog Ring rose up to let Tristan step out from beneath it.

"There!" said Bop Shoowah, happily. "I said that all would be well if you could work with the Moog Ring. My Lady Electrika would have been pleased! Yes, Manchild, it is time…"

He didn't have time to finish. A noise rose from far below. Yeah Yeah opened his scaly wings and buzzed out of the door to investigate it. The approaching red light percolated through the coloured window of the Moog Room and suddenly became darker. They all went to the window and gazed out.

Nothing could be seen except a perceptible blackening

of the sky.

"Probably just the oncoming lapse-light," Tristan concluded. But then, a terrible cry pierced their ears, and Yeah Yeah came yelping back into the room.

A wind grew. Suddenly, billowing, brewing heavy clouds began boiling up a storm. The wind started to blow fiercely into a gale, tossing clouds about.

"You must turn the tape and switch it on, at the fastest speed you must be gone," Scherzo anxiously said to Tristan.

Torrents of noise and rain were now falling from the sky. Then, the rain froze to rock-size hail and an amplified moaning expanded the cascade of noise; filling everything with frenzy.

"It's an illusion!" Tristan insisted, nervously. "I know it is – I've been told so."

"This is no illusion, young friend," said Bop Shoowah, greatly concerned. "It is the angry coming of the Sound Reaper himself."

Tristan realised this truth. With frightened excitement, he hurriedly turned over the golden tape. The air became darker and darker until the only light was vivid streaks of lightning in the sky with dense blackness in between. The sleet had turned into a torrent of flaming jagged arrows and the whooshing noise of fire crackled furiously with the crash of lightning and thunder.

"You must go!" cried Bop Shoowah, desperately. "The Sound Reaper has turned all his energies to preventing your departure. Yet, for all his violence, he cannot harm me now; though you will surely perish." He drew quick nervous breaths.

"I can go!" Tristan shouted above all the chaotic turmoil but what about you, Scherzo?"

"He does not want me, you are the prey of Cacophony!" Scherzo cried.

The window cracked into splinters and the noise that

gushed through was like a thousand hammers crashing onto metal then smashing into glass. Tristan dropped Melody's gem in shock. The walls started splitting and stones fell; one just missed smashing onto his head.

He was more frightened than he had ever been before. It was as if the whole world was being blackened and turned upside down. He could hardly think and was finding it difficult to breathe. Then, he heard a now unseen Bop Shoowah yell frantically, "To do great things, a man must live as though he were about to die! And you are, Manchild! It is you he wants. Return or all will be lost!"

In the billowing gloom. Tristan could see a large green Eye exalting in a blazing painful fire as part of the wall fell away. A huge and terrible dark form in a flaming chariot crashed into the tower.

Tristan couldn't move! He let out scream after scream; for the ultimate fear was now upon him.

*In the middle rose a tall tower shaped remarkably
like a Guitar and it was formed from craggy bluish rock.*

9

A Strange Dream

Tristan woke to find himself lying in bed. He rubbed his eyes. Thankfully, someone else must have pressed the player button and the fading made it seem like it all had been a bad dream. A familiar odour filled his nostrils.

"You alright, son?" his father asked as he came in his dressing gown, smoking his pipe. "You gave out a cry just then! Bad dream or something?"

Had it all been simply a strange dream? Tristan felt dazed but he saw his father was waiting for a reply. 'Make it simple,' Tristan decided. "Yes, Dad," he said without much conviction. "It must have been...I must have had a bad dream or something."

"Don't worry your head about it, son. Breakfast will be ready in ten minutes or so. Get yourself dressed and come to the cookhouse door!" He gave a reassuring smile and, putting another light to the overfull bowl of his pipe, left to finish dressing.

As the door closed, Tristan felt a deep bitter disappointment take hold of him. "All a dream!" he sighed in disbelief, throwing back the bedclothes with disgruntled frustration. A moment later, all such feelings fled – he was still fully clothed, though his clothes were somewhat grimy and dusty as they would be after a long journey on foot.

Excitedly, he got up and there, on the floor, was his tape player where he had dropped it upon his return. The magic tape was still inside.

Hurriedly, Tristan got undressed and put on fresh clothes, covering his bruises.

At breakfast, he had to concentrate to eat absolutely anything at all; thoughts crowded each other, filling every compartment of his mind as he shovelled bacon and baked beans distractedly into his mouth.

He simply couldn't understand how all his adventures in Audia had apparently taken place in only one night of *his* world's time. He decided that either the magic tape had arranged it so or that Audia's measurement of time was vastly different from Lumio's.

Anyway, he couldn't think about that too much. He had a more pressing engagement – namely retrieving the Golden Metronome of Harmony. 'Fancy it being in old Moley's house!' he smiled to himself. It would certainly make his task easier but, remembering Cacophony, the Sound Reaper, he shuddered and pursed his lips recalling how brave he had been in the other Sphere. 'I'll have to be just as brave here!'

"Tristy, why are you rushing so much?" his mother asked. "You'll get a gobbledy-goop in your stomach!"

"Because I'll be late for school."

"My eye and Betty Martin you will, scatter-brain!" his mother gave a little laugh. "Today is Saturday. Anyone would have thought you'd been asleep all week."

Tristan uneasily swallowed his last mouthful of bacon and baked beans. 'That means old Moley will be at home!' This would make things rather more complicated.

Tristan jumped up from the breakfast table and was about to run to get things ready when, "And where do you think you're gallivanting off to, Tristy?" his mother asked in an 'I've-got-something-for-you-to-do' voice. "Because, I've

84

got something for you to do!"

"Well," sighed his father, rising from the table. "I've got to go to the office to deliver some timesheets and a redundancy short-list that I checked last night." He took his pipe from his mouth and gave Mrs. Smith a peck on the cheek.

"O.K., love. I've got a client visiting later, so I'll meet you for lunch," his wife replied as he sauntered through the door, lighting his pipe and leaving an aromatic trail of smoke from his gently glowing ready-rubbed behind.

"That's great." And poking his head back into the kitchen, "Be a good boy," he told Tristan.

"Aren't I always?" Tristan grinned ruefully.

After Tristan helped dry up the breakfast things, his mother asked him if he'd like to come into town with her. And, after she'd shown her client round a new flat, join his father and her for lunch. Tristan declined saying, "I thought I'd watch football in the park." So, as he got his recorder from his bedroom, his mother cut him some cucumber and tomato sandwiches.

Tristan set off down Spring Street. Mr. Lampeter's house was in Winter Walk which was on the other side of town. To get there, he would have to cut across the park, so he hadn't completely lied to his mother.

Tristan was so absorbed in his thoughts he didn't notice that a large black cat, with one enormous green eye, was following him as he walked along.

As the cat slipped behind cars and trees unnoticed, its ominous green eye kept moving from Tristan to the passers-by; waiting for an opportunity when the boy would be alone. The Eye kept surveillance on him – like a security camera in a large store. But the cat's purpose lay very far from Tristan's security.

At last, the Eye saw its chance. As Tristan turned off into a cul-de-sac to the right of August Avenue, the cat bounded and pounced right in front of him, stopping the astonished boy who froze with curious shock and surprise. The big cat cast a swift glance upward and, its eyes fixed on Tristan, was like green fire.

"I….I know who….you are!" Tristan stuttered, terrified from his head to his toes. If only he hadn't lost Melody's gem!

The cat's eye and ears worked together, revealing a build-up of boundless anger and its whole body was quivering as if electricity was passing powerfully through it. The air between the cat and Tristan seemed to vibrate.

"Turn back!" A voice menaced as the cat's eye blazed with lurid flames and its sharp white teeth shone. Its ears went back furiously. It gnashed its sharp, pointy teeth as large claws stood out at stark full length on every paw. All its fur stood up on end, making it seem even larger as its back arched. Then, with a terrible scream and tail lashing furiously, it leapt at Tristan!

"Cacophony! Leave me alone!" cried the boy, closing his eyes and waiting for the terrible moment of tearing impact. Nothing happened. Wearily, Tristan slowly opened his eyes. The cat was nowhere to be seen.

'I wonder why he ran away.' Tristan mused nervously to himself. 'Perhaps he was just trying to scare me off recovering the Metronome.' He pursed his lips and screwed up his eyes with determination. 'Well, he didn't scare me. I won't knuckle under. For once I have real friends and I will help them. I will!'

The last 'I will' came out rather loudly. An old lady taking in her one precious milk bottle from the dirty doorstep gave Tristan a rather funny look. She cradled a small black kitten that meowed affectionately in her left arm.

Tristan carried on, eating a cucumber and tomato sandwich as if to take his mind off things. He recalled what Scherzo had once said to him when they were wandering in Jazz. 'Many forms the devourer can appear in, changing as easily as a snake sloughs off its skin.' Tristan shuddered.

'Hum. Don't like the sound of that at all!'

He climbed over some railings and onto December Drive. Soon, he was in Four Seasons Park. Cautiously, he kept out of sight as best he could. Fearful but resolute, he ventured across the greens, slipping behind trees and any cover wherever possible. He was sweating profusely. He could hear the sounds of a football match being played – how nice and ordinary it seemed. He had never before understood how good 'everyday' things could be. Not far away, he saw the old boat keeper repairing one of his boats.

Suddenly, the old boat keeper turned to Tristan and gazed at him. Tristan felt a curious recognition in his eyes. "Come here," the old boat keeper beckoned to him, his bright blue eyes sparkling. "Come here. I have seen. I think I can help you."

Tristan made a move towards him, but all at once, there was a whistle of breeze that grew into a loud thumping windy noise. The wind began bringing down large quantities of leaves, which its gusts took and whirled into spiral pillars forming prison bars around him. A shapeless shadow spreading itself before Tristan began to take form and a tall man stepped from behind a bush. The man had a rather ramshackle face with skin the colour of impure yellow wax blotched with dirt and pockmarks. He wore a dirty black patch over one eye. The other eye was abnormally large, glittering a luminous green.

"LEAVE ALONE!" the man threatened in an animal snarl, raising a large, grim fist to strike the boy.

"Cacophony! Don't!" Tristan cowered.

To his astonishment, the evil man vanished at once, taking the leaf prison and noisy wind with him.

For a moment, Tristan stood puzzled, thinking hard. He remembered what Vina had said about the Eye of Obi Aleatoree. 'Simply say, 'Cacophony' and I will help compel it to return.' Perhaps this held true even in Lumio so that when he said the evil one's name, Cacophony was forced to return to Audia.

'That is it!' Tristan reassured himself. 'The black cat didn't just mean to warn me off, it had to go because I said its real name out loud, destroying its disguise!'

He saw the old boat keeper coming toward him but Tristan wouldn't be stopped. He ran off through the Park down Christmas Crescent and into Winter Walk. He stopped at the corner and, leaning thoughtfully on a lamppost, contemplated the best course of action. 'How can I get in?' Mr. Lampeter's house was a fairly large Victorian semi-detached home with a cellar as well as an attic.

He decided the best course of action was to get into the house through the cellar – it would be dark and would therefore lend ample opportunity to hide if someone heard him.

It started raining and, with a final look around, Tristan crept up to open one of the cellar door flaps. He slowly lowered himself into the darkness.

10

Lampeter's 'Home Sweet Home'

Although the cellar was coal-black, Tristan could just make out a crack of light high in the right hand wall. He decided it was light slicing through the bottom of the cellar door, so the stairs must be beneath the strip of light.

Trying as hard as he could to not bump into or knock anything over, he bumped into several objects and knocked over what felt like a long sharp saw – a saw that cut him! 'Typical!' he complained to himself as he listened to hear if there were any sounds of movement upstairs. None...except a sort of muffled whisper that seemed to be in the cellar with him. He waited. When nothing came of it, he carried on.

As last, his foot knocked against something familiar. He bent over and touched a wooden stop. He crawled noiselessly on his hands and knees up the stairs and tried to peep through the crack at the bottom of the door. All he could see were the beginnings of an old red carpet and the bottom of some chair legs.

Quietly, he got up and with a tentative motion, fingered the metal door latch. His heart 'thumped' with his measured movement as he raised the latch. After accomplishing this, he pushed the door slightly ajar. It creaked a little. Tristan cringed. He glimpsed through. There was no one in sight! He let the door open until it was wide enough ajar for him to slip through.

Tristan sucked on his bleeding cut and, as the blood made his mouth taste slightly metallic and slightly rustic, he looked ahead of him. The hall was quite narrow and fairly long. The first thing he noticed was a small tapestry picture with 'Home Sweet Home' embroidered on it. It was hung on a pale cream wall. A table with a semi-circular red top on which resided a pale cream telephone was below it and, appropriately enough, he noticed a pale cream address book on the small table.

Tristan slid from behind the cellar door and then shut it carefully. He turned on 'cat-feet' and was about to place his right foot on the first step when, "Smith! What on earth are you doing here?" Tristan froze in his tracks when he heard the all-too-familiar voice. Instantly, he turned to see 'Moley' Lampeter turning away from him.

"Oh, humbug!" Tristan sighed.

"Well, Laddie. This is a surprise! I'm sure you have an explanation why you're creeping thief-like about my home." Mr. Lampeter sounded very serious. "Come in here and tell me about it!"

Tristan followed the teacher into the front room which had the appearance of a study with three walls completely lined with hardback books of various ages, conditions, and colours. In the middle of the room, there was a large writing desk with a chair nudging it on either side.

"You had best sit down, Smith!" the teacher said, keeping his back to Tristan. Tristan reluctantly obeyed. He decided that although he hadn't told his parents about Audia because it might put them in danger, it would be best to tell Mr. Lampeter the truth. He probably wouldn't believe him but something gave him the feeling that he just might.

"Look, sir, I know this all seems strange but I can explain. At least I think I can," he paused. "But..."

"But what, Laddie?"

"You'll think I'm balmy, sir, but it's the simple truth!"

"The truth is never simple, Smith. The world is full of strange things. It's all like riding a horse in search of a horse."

"Pardon?" Tristan was slightly bemused.

"It's how you look at things that matters in the end, isn't it?" the teacher said. "Things that don't seem to make sense on the surface may have great truth and logic underneath. Tell me your story – even if it seems 'balmy'. I'll look for the truth beneath."

So, as quickly as he could and with mounting excitement, Tristan related his coming to and journey in the world of Audia. He told him of Harmony, the Grand City of Tranquility, of Scherzo, of the Queen and Conn Ductor, of his mission, and "The evilness of ...."

"Enough, Laddie!" Mr. Lampeter said abruptly. "Stop galloping around at the top of your voice. I have heard enough!" Then, in a softer tone, "I know all I need to. Yes, Smith, your 'nonsense' is most interesting. Like a bladeless sword with no handle. Ha ha!"

"It isn't nonsense – please be serious!" Tristan began to feel that there was something rather disconcerting about the teacher's manner. He watched the back of his teacher for further reaction. 'Moley' was wringing his hands together as if trying to control some emotion.

Then, Mr. Lampeter came out from behind his desk, his back still turned to the boy, and started pacing the room looking at books. "The more you know, tin tear drop, the less you think you know!" he began. "It's all a circle; always bringing us back in the end."

Tristan shifted uneasily in his seat as the teacher halted for a moment, then resumed his pacing.

"The little you know you owe to your ignorance! It was a dark and stormy night," he began, "and a thief turned to his accomplice, 'Tell me a story,' he said and so, the accomplice began, 'It was a dark and stormy night!'"

91

Tristan was now very uncomfortable indeed. Mr. Lampeter was not acting 'Moley.' Indeed! He was not even acting like Mr. Lampeter at all! Tristan began to realise that he had noticed something odd when he had first been discovered – he had caught a glimpse of Mr. Lampeter's glasses before he turned. They had seemed somehow strange but he had been too worried to think this over before. Now, the recognition flickered.

"Mr. Lampeter…" Tristan began, cautiously but didn't have time to finish. In a flash, the teacher stuck a large piece of masking tape over Tristan's mouth and busily tied his hands together behind his back.

"That'll cease your senseless verbal scribbling!" he said in a voice completely altered to gruff wickedness. He stepped in front of the startled, dismayed boy and stared at him through glasses tinted dark green. He twitched and a spasm took hold of him as if a huge power rippled through his being. Taking off the tinted spectacles, he sent them smashing to the floor. Beneath, on the evilly transformed face - no eyes or sockets – just green flames flashing from the blazing eyeball that hovered in front of his fiery forehead.

His voice was a confusion of many horrible sounds, out of which words percolated menacingly like a crowd of demons talking the same words, only each one slightly out-of-time with the others.

Tristan, unable to speak his name, was at last completely in Cacophony's power.

11

The Sound Reaper's Scheme

"Now, I have you, Manchild!" Cacophony gloated in his several voices – out-of-tune and out-of-key. "An interesting story you told, eh! Nonsense, little fool! The only nonsense is your resistance. What shall be shall be! Didn't really expect to better me, did you? Ha-ha! Even if my power is diminished in your Sphere, I am yet more powerful than any mortal kind!"

The whole study was alive with dancing shadows cast by lurid green fire. It was as Tristan had once imagined hell might be like.

"Idiot! If you had left well enough alone, I would not have had to ensnare you like this. Now, burglar, you know too much and may find out more!" His voice filled Tristan's head, making it ache terribly. "I have the Interruptor, maggot. I have brought it to show you before I return to Din!" He flourished a very large flame-shaped rod that glowed darkly and made Tristan tremble sick with pain like a frightful migraine.

"That fool Conn Ductor – how I knew him before! The slime, always wily, but now I am greater than he or any Waltz Lord could ever be. I found the Interruptor hidden deep in the Decibel Pass. I would have found it sooner if not for your cursed distraction. Still, ha!" He laughed and held the Interruptor high in triumph, enjoying the fore taste of greater victories to come. Tristan felt as though his head was going to explode.

"Now, I shall return to Audia and deliver this to the Discords. Yes, Din shall get the leader it deserves! I save them so they shall serve me – I need servants. Before, I served but now I knew that there would come a time when I would be Overlord. Obtaining Aleatoree, Eye of Obi, was but the first leap to my position of ultimate power."

Cacophony's terrible words whipped through Tristan's brain mercilessly. He ceased to understand much of what was being said. It was just so much throbbing noise. Tristan tried not to pass out, but Cacophony was unrelenting in his vainglory.

"Would that the Concord Race had but one head so that I could easily chop it off. But once they and their precious Metronome are destroyed, Harmony will be ruined and Conn Ductor killed by inches so he suffers most. Then, all the lands of Audia shall be mine. I will put my servants, the Discords, in control of Audia and, then worm – I shall turn my attention to your Sphere – 'Sweet Lumio!' Yes, it too shall become my dominion. Your world in its 'proud' gowns will grovel at my feet. Ha! I shall be Overlord of all! From the first howls in the morning to the last screams at night – I shall control everything!"

His evil eye flamed with greed. The noise of insane laughter splashed at all of Tristan's senses like razor blades in his mind and, with the strain and blinding light, Tristan at last lost consciousness....

....Like attempting to flick away thick tentacles from sticking your eyelids down, Tristan came round, his head still buzzing with dull throbbing pain. He was now no longer in the study but in the dark of the cellar.

He was still firmly trussed up, the tape remained binding his lips together and preventing any sound from coming from them. He was helpless! Tears rolled down his flushed, trembling cheeks. He felt lost and completely abandoned. What could he do? Then, he remembered his cut and the long sharp saw. He could see the light still slicing through the space at the bottom of the cellar door. Tristan tried with all his concentration to determine exactly where it was that he had knocked the saw over.

He couldn't stand up; he couldn't move his arms or legs but he could roll. And roll he did – banging into everything except the saw that he so longed to find. He was becoming desperate. Then, he felt something bite into his tied hands, cutting him. Instead of feeling pain, he felt pleasure. Tristan immediately manipulated himself into a proper position and started rolling and rubbing his bonds as hard as he could against the teeth of the blade. The rope started to fray and loosen when, with a flurry of noise and green sparks, Cacophony returned – still partially in his Lampeter form, though the evil beneath was bursting out more and more all the time – being too great to contain. In the light of the lurid flames, Tristan could see the real Mr. and Mrs. Lampeter firmly trussed up in the corner – both unconscious.

"So, Manchild," the Sound Reaper began, in his voices laden with malevolence, making Tristan's head pulsate once more, "I have returned the Interruptor to Din. Even now, Loud Crashbang and his armies of Anxiety are preparing to march on Harmony. The other Waltz Lords sought to stop my rise but when Conn Ductor is destroyed, my victory will be complete! You cannot prevent this! However, Manchild, in this Sphere you can benefit yourself."

Again, Tristan felt his head was going to violently pop apart. 'Whatever I do I must not pass out!' He gritted his teeth as he worked his bonds slowly behind his back, sawing them looser and looser.

"You see, Manchild, I cannot attain full power as long as the accursed Metronome exists. Forever it has been a burden on me! I cannot destroy it. I cannot bear to be near it. Even now it weakens me. The Discords cannot destroy it – it weakens them also and it is thus protected. Only one who is pure, a stranger to greed and evil, a lover of that foul thing that is music, can destroy it. One such as you! All you have to do is stop the time pendulum. Once it is halted, its protective power will be gone and I can complete the destruction. If you do this thing, I will make you Lord of Lumio! You will be the most powerful of your kind! I have had servants in your Sphere before but with the destruction of the Metronome, you will gain world power as they could not!" He paused. His eye shot bands of green about, colouring the cellar with eerie luminescence.

"But, if you refuse to help me, I will exterminate you and all those close to you. After Harmony is blasted apart, I shall return. Give me your answer then. To make sure that you do not escape, I will destroy the recorder and tape so that you can never journey to Audia again without my consent."

Cacophony paced quickly forward. Tristan's pain was unbearable – he felt himself being drawn into the dizzy whirlpool of unconsciousness. He had to act now! Pulling one hand free, he ripped the tape from his mouth.

"Cacophony!" he screamed at the top of his voice. There was a thunderous rumble, a cry of rage, a flare of green flame that singed some of Tristan's hair, and the Sound Reaper was gone!!!!

"Thank goodness!" Tristan sighed, his head still pounding as if someone with a hammer was banging on the inside of his skull. He hurriedly and shakily undid the remainder of his bonds and went over to where Mr. and Mrs. Lampeter were, loosening their ropes so that when they came around they could easily work themselves free.

He then hurried in the darkness up the stairs, continually saying, "Cacophony... Cacophony .... Cacophony!" Over and over again out loud in case the wicked one should attempt to return.

Through the Victorian hall and up another flight of stairs he sped. He was in the attic soon. His mind was fully aware that time was running out and the evil army was marching to destroy Harmony. In the left hand corner were the storage boxes that he had seen while in the Moog Ring. He rushed over and, one by one, removed them.

Suddenly, a golden glow bathed him in a warm, refreshing light. Soon, he was staring at the biggest, most beautifully carved Metronome he had ever seen – he had only ever seen one before in the music room of St. Julian's but it would be like comparing a rotten lump of wood to the largest, most precious gem that had ever existed.

As the pendulum kept rhythmic time from side to side, its ticking filled Tristan with ease and strength. His headache went completely as a new feeling of life surged through his body.

Then, "It must have been burglars, Chota," said a 'Moley' voice.

"Yes, Bufee, but I can't seem to recall a thing that happened..."

There was a pause, then, "Henry, look! The step ladder is up and a strange glow is coming from the attic. Whether ape or angel, there is someone up there. For goodness sake, Buffee, phone the police!"

"Yes, Chota, of course!"

The shrill, frantic voice subsided into the sound of hurrying feet scurrying down the stairs and a phone being dialed.

Tristan tried and tried to pick up the Golden Metronome but it was far too heavy. He couldn't shift it an inch. So, thinking quickly, he turned his tape over, switched it on, and then wrapped his arms round part of the Metronome and clung on as tightly as he could.

His evil eye flamed with greed.

12

Anxiety Must Be Stopped

Everything was silent. No flame flickered in the great Bell-fire. The Bell-room's colours were all washed out. He was back with Conn Ductor and anxious to see him.

"I hope I'm not too late!"

But, as Tristan fully arrived, the Golden Metronome to which he clung tightly still shone out more brightly than ever, bathing the room in a rich, golden sea of light, frowning the grey forever.

Tristan heard someone sigh deeply, as if awakening from a long sleep. Conn Ductor raised himself slowly from his large Bell-backed chair.

"You have done well, Manchild," said the old Waltz Lord, his strength returning under the reviving influence of the Metronome. "It is joyous to see you again," he sang out and with a wave of his hand, a vigorous fire sprang up brightly in the grate.

"I'm very glad to be back!" Tristan smiled.

"However, time runs out," Conn Ductor said, seriously. "I must replace our Golden Music-Giver." With that, he picked up the Metronome as if it were as light as marshmallow.

"Goodness, how strong!" Tristan exclaimed.

Conn Ductor turned and, beckoning Tristan to follow, strode hurriedly out of the room. Tristan followed on his heels as best he could. Down the high musical corridor they went and down the marble steps into the Bell Garden. Tristan's thoughts turned to Scherzo but he knew now was not the time for questions.

Golden beams radiated everywhere from the ticking Metronome - life, light, music, and colour were restored. Even so, Tranquility seemed deserted. 'Ask no questions - get no lies!' his mother always said. Conn Ductor wasn't his mother, so, "Where is everybody?" Tristan asked.

"Our people went to their homes to fade away with their families," replied the hurrying Waltz Lord. The thought of 'Fading away with one's family' struck Tristan as rather depressing.

"But, they shall come forth and rejoice when *this* is restored," Conn Ductor said. "We owe you a great debt, Manchild!"

"It was nothing!" Tristan grinned wryly, knowing that it was almost everything as like a refreshing tide flowing over a parched shore. The Metronome's energy brought back the splendid life of Harmony.

A climax of Fugue-birds rose from nearby Lyre bushes and burst into the lightening sky, circling as they sang their melodious songs. Tiny white clouds blossomed in the blue sky, waving on stems of sunlight. The smoke-grey leaves of the music trees changed – their colours returning and assuming a rich and splendid hue as the leaves played tunes with the breeze and fell in celebration from their tranquil branches like a snowfall of precious stones. Concords rushed, cheering from their homes into the Palace Avenue of statues.

Conn Ductor was increasing his pace in the final stretch. Tristan could see Queen Rhapsody and Princess Melody sitting on the Throne at the foot of the Gem Goddess.

Queen Rhapsody rose and took gliding steps to meet Conn Ductor. "Oh, praise to you sweet Manchild." She rejoiced as Conn Ductor purposefully put the Metronome down.

Tristan smiled as she turned and sang a gloriously high-pitched note. Immediately, thirty Fugues swirled down from the sky, hovering just in reach of her hand. She gave each one a golden cord that they each took in their silver beaks. These thirty golden strands formed one rope, and the Fugues bound the rope around the Metronome. With a wave of her hand, the command was given and the Fugues rose and gently placed the Metronome in the left hand of the Gem Goddess; releasing the cords as they did so.

At once, it was as if the whole huge statue came to life - it sparkled all the colours Tristan could imagine - and some that he couldn't! There was a glorious peal of bells as the whole city was bathed in a golden-diamond light.

Melody ran up and happily kissed Tristan on the cheek. "I'm so happy to see you again, Manchild!" she said.

"Thank you," Tristan replied. "It's good to see you as well!"

Queen Rhapsody climbed onto the platform in front of the throne. "Now, my Concords!" she said to the crowds. "The great wrong that was committed has been set to right. The Manchild has done us a glorious service."

The crowd cheered - a loud musical hum of thanks was given three times.

"We are forever in his debt - however...." she stressed in a grave voice that caused the gathered Concords to fall silent, "time for rejoicing has not yet come. The Discords and the evil one are in league still and are moving in to destroy us. We must act swiftly! Prince Staccato will tell the battle plan."

A tall Concord in crimson and cream with embellishments of bronze trumpets on his armour strode forward. He stood by Queen Rhapsody.

"Lord Loud Crashbang's army of Anxiety approaches!" he began, sternly surveying the crowd. "Even now, a Fugue has brought word that Din's forces are on the borders of Modal Sands. We must muster our forces of Opera and engage them before they cross the Baroque Plains. All Valleys of Harmony are preparing now that Music has been re-given. We shall march before dusk and travel beneath the cloak of lapse-light. We shall never be overcome!"

The crowd cheered and then dispersed rapidly to help with the preparations of battle. Tristan turned to Melody, "Where is Scherzo?" he asked, no longer able to contain the question. "What happened to him?"

"We don't know." Melody sighed sadly, softly touching his hand with hers as if to compensate.

"Manchild," said Conn Ductor, "we know nothing of Scherzo's exact whereabouts. However, if he survived the Sound Reaper's wrath, which I feel he did, then the Golden Metronome will give him reviving strength at this very moment and Scherzo, at his best, is a match for a dozen Discords!"

"But what if he's captured or, what if ... if ...?"

"Manchild, Manchild!" said Conn Ductor softly, putting a calming hand on Tristan's shoulder. "There is no time for this now. I have fears that Cacophony has plans to settle an old debt by attacking Tranquility whilst the Forces of Harmony are battling Din. He will seek revenge from both of us. You must return to your world. It is no longer safe for you here."

"What made it so safe here for me before, with creatures like that Rubats and Obi Aleatoree about?" Tristan asked. "Look, I want to stay! I have a right to!" he urged, impressing even himself.

Melody smiled at his insistence. The Queen was about to say something when a Concord in green and gold armour, with white violins patterned around the edges, strode purposefully forward. Prince Staccato followed.

"Your Tranquil Majesty, the combined Opera awaits your command!"

"Of course, Prince Crescendo!" And, giving Tristan a radiant smile, she left. Melody took hold of Tristan's hand, her wish that he stay having been granted.

"So be it!" Conn Ductor frowned. "I ask of you, though, to do exactly as I say. Now, follow me!"

With that, he turned and hurried back to the Bell Palace. Tristan and Melody followed, hand-in-hand. Once inside, they climbed flight after flight of steps until they reached what Conn Ductor called his 'Preparation Room,' that reminded Tristan of the inside of a huge, purple glass bell. It was positioned almost at the very top of the building. Tristan could see for miles in all directions through its coloured glass and, in all directions, he could see Concords in many different coloured armour, mounted or on foot and laden with all manner of musical instruments. The Concords' steeds were like deer of silvery green or silvery brown with great golden Lyre antlers.

"Haven't your Concords any weapons?" Tristan asked.

"They are holding them, Manchild." Melody, laughed gently and pointed at the musical instruments.

"Oh, I see. Of course," Tristan said, but wondered how effective flutes would be against the fierce Discords.

Conn Ductor leant over a large book, humming things to himself. Tristan could see that there was no writing on the book pages - but the pages were filled with musical symbols and scales.

Tristan and Melody sat down on a long comfortable couch fashioned like a tubular bell. Peering below, Tristan could just make out Queen Rhapsody majestically stepping up to Prince Crescendo of the Rearguard, who knelt. The Queen then placed a ring of orange bells around his neck.

Prince Crescendo rose and, kissing the Tranquil Queen's lovely hand, hummed a sad, touching tune of farewell; then mounted his silvery steed.

Thus, the last of the brave Opera army of Harmony left Tranquility.

Tristan was beginning to feel heavy-eyed and drowsy. But, before he finally fell asleep, above the sound of distant marching he heard an uplifting musical voice proclaim, "Anxiety SHALL be stopped!"

*Golden beams radiated everywhere from the ticking Metronome -
life, light, music, and colour were restored.*

13

As Music Moves, Noise Creeps In

Tristan didn't know how long he had been asleep. 'Must have been some little time.' For lapse-light was almost over when he awoke. He could hear a humming noise and when he glanced over the sleeping Princess, he saw that Conn Ductor was still intensely contemplating his book.

"So you have awoken, Manchild!" said the old Waltz Lord without looking up from his studies.

"Yes, thank you," replied the boy, getting up with a stretch and a yawn. "What are you doing?"

"You would not understand, Manchild. Let us say that I am making preparations for Cacophony's attack that I know must come." Conn Ductor thoughtfully turned a page over.

"Cacophony!" Tristan said with a shiver. "I can't forget the monstrous things he said when he had me captured in Mr. Lampeter's house."

Conn Ductor looked up from his book and gazed curiously at the boy. "What did the Sound Reaper say, Manchild?" he asked very seriously.

Tristan had not expected to have to relate the horrible experience. He could not remember everything but what he could remember, he told to the Waltz Lord, who seemed more and more interested in what Tristan was saying. Every so often he would say, "Are you quite sure he said that?"

However, there was one part in particular that seemed to interest, in fact excite, Conn Ductor. "So long I served, then I discovered the evil Eye, yet the other Waltz Lords sought to stop me."

"Are you certain he said 'other' Waltz Lords?" Conn Ductor urged.

"Yes! Quite sure!"

"Other Waltz Lords!" Conn Ductor placed his hands on Tristan's shoulders. "It was destined you remain with me for you have provided a vital clue as to how I may battle and overcome the evil one. You have added the one missing part to solve a mystery that has long troubled me. I refused at first to believe it could be! Ah! Poor Inno Vator - yet Comm Poser is the true tragedy!" Conn Ductor suddenly thrust a bottle of pink liquid into Tristan's hands.

"Drink this, my boy!" he said. "You must be hungry."

"But, Conn Ductor, I don't under....!"

"No time! No time!" Conn Ductor proclaimed. "I must prepare something quickly! Stay here!" With that, and talking excitedly to himself, he left.

Melody woke. They waited for some time but, after a while and preoccupied with curiosity, Melody insisted they go down. Tristan agreed.

"Stay clear!" shouted Conn Ductor, lifting up a bell of orange-frosted crystal about the size of an armchair and planting it on a pedestal at the top of the steps. He squinted an eye, measuring to be sure that it was directly in line with the great Golden Metronome and, sure enough, a diamond beam of burnished gold briefly bathed the orange bell in a luminous glow.

"Perfect!" he exclaimed. "I am almost prepared!"

This would have heartened Tristan to no end except that the 'almost' seemed rather ominous, especially since at that moment, there was a loud cry that split the soft air. Several

Fugue creatures flew in chortling panic from the Garden of the great Bell Tree.

"It has begun!" Conn Ductor said, frowning.

There was the noise of crashing, clanging, and iron grating. There was a fearsome, angry cry, as a Headache of twenty or so armed and evil-looking Discords rode into the beautiful Avenue of Gem Statues. They were dressed in dirty brown and grey armour with dirty brown and yellow helmets sporting black plumes. Their faces were all covered by squinting, leering, lecherous, dribbling, jackal-jawed, weasel-mouthed, and shrew-faced masks.

The one that appeared to be their leader was smaller than the rest. He was dressed in dirty red and black with a pair of broken yellow wings on his helmet. On his grimy breastplate were two jagged lines of lightning with a set of barred, grinning teeth in the middle that were all carved in livid green. His evil squint-eyed mask displayed a dribbling mouth of shark teeth from which a long yellow wolf-like tongue hung.

The Headache's mounts were like ostriches except their heads and mouths were those of crocodiles filled with sharp uneven teeth. The mounts were of different shades of grimy purple.

"An advanced troop." Conn Ductor didn't even seem surprised. "Come a swift way, riding both day and lapse-light to pick off easy prey. Ha! Easy prey! Into the Palace you two."

"What of Mother?" Melody asked, anxiously.

"She will be alright," he answered. "Just do as I say!" Melody went in with Tristan.

The leader of the Discords had turned his mount. The Headache halted, preparing to attack Queen Rhapsody who, on her Crystal Throne, remained seemingly unaffected by their sudden arrival. The wicked leader raised his hand and was about to blurt out a command when, "I know you!" Conn Ductor's mocking voice filled the air.

The leader lowered his arm and turned his head about. "Do ya, Gob-clot?" said the Discord in an ugly voice.

"Yes, 'little' Discord, you are Buzz Deafening, Loud Crashbang's stupid son sent on an easy mission to pillage Tranquility whilst our army is absent. Imbecile. A woman of Harmony is worth any ten soldiers of Din.

The Discord trembled with rage. "Oooo the 'eck do ya think y'are, eh? I'll dispatch ya right now, puke-ball!"

"Fool!" taunted Conn Ductor. His voice echoed like thunder. "Did your 'great' leader not think that I would remain? Or has Cacophony chosen to keep silent so that he might leave the battle between him and me for later, unhampered by your meddling? Well, this is a bad day for you, Nincompoop. I have kept my real presence secret for so long from Din but now you, ones with no conscience, shall know me for what I am!"

"Conscience! I have a clean conscience!" screamed Buzz Deafening. "I haven't used it once! 'Do away with 'im!"

Seven Discords from the Headache reared their snapping purple mounts and charged toward Conn Ductor, swirling jagged black weapons in the air which gave off the most frightful noise, making Tristan feel dizzy. Melody winced but stood firm.

Conn Ductor remained calm and, walking down the steps, stood right in the path. He waved his hands in the air, which vibrated with wonderful music at his silent command.

The charging Discords' helmets turned to molten metal on their masked heads and their Noise blades melted like grimy candles in their claw-like hands. Before they came within fifteen feet of the stern Waltz Lord they fell senselessly to the ground! With distressed gasps for air, their two-legged steeds turned and fled in all directions.

"Ugh!" screamed Buzz Deafening. "'Owed ya do it, eh?"

Conn Ductor stared at him with powerful, frowning eyes, giving out a warning that the Discord would not heed.

"'Way with 'im!" he cried again, almost choking with wrath. "Skedaddle and croak 'im."

Seven more Discords charged on their snapping steeds, although this time with a reluctance that was visible. Conn Ductor shook his head and waved his hands to weave the air about him into a magical tune, playing the secrets of the atmosphere. The Discord's weapons and armour melted away again. And, with cries of sorrow and disillusionment, they fell unconscious from their fleeing mounts.

Buzz Deafening suddenly pulled his mount round with a vicious tug of the reins. "Forget about moron-mouth, my warts inherit 'is nose. Grab 'er." He pointed a furious trembling finger towards Queen Rhapsody. "Grab 'er, the accursed Slimecord Queen!" He whirled his noise-maker savagely in the air and charged towards her with the remainder of the Headache troop resentfully in tow. Queen Rhapsody remained firmly seated on her throne.

The closer the Discords charged, cursing and noise-making, the brighter the Great Metronome shone. The closer the Discords rode, the more they were bathed in diamond light and the more they seemed to grow fainter, as if in the process of being erased by some invisible rubber. They were fading away under its influence.

"Eh! Wot the 'eck's 'appening?" cried one of the increasingly insubstantial Discords.

"What's that Clanger Nob?" yelled Buzz Deafening, and that was the last noise he ever made. Both he and his steed dissolved into a shimmering rod of light that suddenly gave off a delightfully harmonious tinkle before vanishing completely.

Clanger Nob, Captain of the Headache, reared up and the rest of the Headache pulled to a jerking halt, as one by one, they too turned to light and sound and vanished in the powerfully harmonic rays of the Great Golden Metronome that was placed in the hands of the Gem Goddess.

"Hoorah!" yelled Melody, running down the steps to the Waltz Lord, who stood thoughtfully gazing as the last Discord that was dispelled.

Tristan beamed beside her. "A victory!" he said triumphantly.

Conn Ductor turned to him with a serious stare, "No, Manchild," he said. "We have not yet won. This has been but a small foretaste of the danger that is too soon to come!"

""Way with 'im!" he cried again, almost choking with wrath. "Skedaddle and croak 'im."

Chapter 14

The Baroque Plains

Prince Crescendo, still bedecked with orange bells, rode the rearguard. Lapse-light finished as he gazed at the Opera army stretching out of sight ahead. He had served in the last Symphonic War. Now, he was Prince and Battle Leader of all Emerald Binary. Yet, he was not happy. He was deeply in love with Queen Rhapsody and he knew she loved him but they could never be joined. It was forbidden that a Tranquil Queen ever have more than one Consort unless there were no heirs.

Queen Rhapsody had an heir – Melody. Yet, if he was to shine as a hero against the enemy, perhaps they would allow that a fearless Queen might, by right, be joined with a hero that had served her land. He swept back a greeny-blue lock of hair that had fallen down across his determined brow and smiled with resolution.

Prince Andante of Sonata rode in mid-formation with his azure and silver armour glittering in the high light that showed up the yellow motif of Flutes. The morning was almost over as he complained to himself that he had not originally been informed of the plan to steal the Interruptor. Prince Crescendo had been made responsible to Queen Rhapsody – but then Prince Crescendo always was!

He took his thoughts off these fruitless ponderings by working out a planned attack against the Discords. He loved working out plans of attack and wondered why nobody let him make them anymore. His last plan of attack in the late Symphonic War had inadvertently led to the death of the Queen's husband, Grand Prince Maestroso – that was why! Yes, but if he could shine in this new conflict, then they would all see that he was the noblest Prince of all.

Prince Staccato of Rondo, proud in colours of crimson and cream with bronze motif trumpets ablaze, rode side by side with Prince Allegro of Ternary in the early afternoon light. Being a great historian and lover of buildings, Staccato's most celebrated moment had been when he had built his tremendous Trumpet Tower in Rondo. At the top of the tower he would gaze over what was and think of what had been. This battle would be one of the most decisive of all – it thrilled him. Yet, the doubt of victory hung on him heavily - he knew more of Cacophony than most!

Prince Allegro of Ternary gazed ahead at the heavy clouds of mid-afternoon and knew a storm was brewing. He was the youngest of the Princes and had a quick, lively mind. His only sorrow was the memory of the death of Prince Forte of Binary, the brother of Prince Crescendo. Prince Forte of Binary lost his life during an ambush in the Modal Sands by Buzz Deafening and a Headache of Discords. Prince Crescendo took Forte's place after these events. Prince Allegro disliked Buzz Deafening more than any other creature in Audia and would have been overjoyed to hear of his fate back in Tranquility.

Prince Allegro was the only one of the Princes that truly wished that Prince Crescendo and Queen Rhapsody could be joined. He knew that Forte would have wished it too. He looked to either side of him. His colours of magenta and mauve, with a motif of silver drums, were overcast by the brewing storm.

Binary's emerald, Ternary's magenta, Sonata's azure and the crimson of Rondo, merged in tight formation as they

112

approached the Baroque plains. In the distance, the turbulent sound of another army could be heard.

"Sing for victory!" cried Prince Staccato, raising an arm and waving it high. A mighty sound filled the air as all Opera joined in the defiant singing and blotting out the distant, approaching noise of Din's Anxiety.

Prince Crescendo of the rear-guard gave his steed, Pibcorn, a slight kick and galloped ahead to the catch up to the Princes Staccato and Allegro. "Let me ride ahead!" he called. "I will see how the situation fares."

"Glory seeker!" Andante muttered to himself.

"But who will take the rear-guard?" Staccato asked.

"I shall!" Allegro ventured.

So, Prince Crescendo rode over the rise in the ground and stared across the Baroque plains, surveying the challenge to be met. He viewed Anxiety fast approaching – ugly and fearsome and in vast numbers. He swiftly turned his steed about and galloped back. "Prepare!" he shouted. "Din will soon be upon us!"

A thousand fluttering flags were raised; some bearing emblems of Ternary's silver drums, some with the bronze trumpet motifs of Rondo, others aglow with the yellow flutes of Sonata. And still others were flying proudly with the white violins of Binary.

Ten thousand glittering instruments were unsheathed and held high. The battle hum turned into the disturbed air as the Opera of Harmony rode down upon the Baroque Plains, where the Anxiety of Din was crashing and thundering into sight.

Lord Loud Crashbang, on his purple two-legged mount, rode at the front of Anxiety. He was arrayed in evil-looking green-black armour and his helmet was threatening with large yellow lightning bolts carved on either side like vultures' wings. He also bore the two carved jagged lightning bolts on his chest and in the middle was carved a grinning mouth of bared teeth with a long, pointed tongue sticking out. His grotesque mask had but one single eye of luminous green in the center with flared wolf-like nostrils below and a dribbling spike-filled mouth with a long green tongue waggling mockingly.

Lord Loud Crashbang was flanked by Baron Dis Traction and Baron Dis Onance in murky brown and livid green respectfully. Dis Traction had a squint-eyed, buck-fanged mask with a broken nose and livid yellow scars. Dis Onance had a dirty mask with Quasimodo eyes at different levels, one high on his scarred forehead, the other beneath his pig-like nose. His mouth was screwed up in a sickly grimace.

The whole of Anxiety wore masks of various gruesome designs and brandished terribly jagged noise-makers as their thousands of slimy tongues moved madly. Prince Andante would have preferred to ambush them in the Helicon Hills but no one would have listened, so he maintained a resentful silence.

The two sides halted.

From Opera, Prince Crescendo rode forth. From Anxiety, Lord Crashbang clanged forward.

"So, ya managed to reach us in time, maggot-brain!" said the Noise Lord. "Well, it won't do ya no good. We'll pummel ya all ta pulp. Ha!" The gruff sound that Crashbang gave off from behind his ugly mask was maliciously mocking.

"We shall see, Crashbang," said Prince Crescendo proudly. "You have never defeated us before. You shall not now!"

"Pah!" grunted Crashbang. "Some say I have a preoccupation with vengeance. We'll see about that when I stuff ya with noises and twist ya all up in a knot! Ha-ha!" His burst of laughter scuttled sideways like a stinking crowd of cockroaches and slobbersides. He spat on the ground. They each rode back to their respective sides.

Before Crescendo had time to report to the three waiting

Princes, a foul Din-bolt burst above his head. With a groan, he fell from his rearing steed. In an instant, the air was full of noise bolts from Anxiety's weapons, jamming the sky with whirling confusion. Many Concords fell, stunned and senseless. Those that were too close had their eardrums shattered and collapsed to the ground.

Then, instruments ready, the Concords retaliated, charging at the treacherous Discords with a rushing scream of sound, breaking wave upon musical wave over the barren, bleak Plains of Baroque. Noise and Music clashed in struggle. The opposing armies were locked in battle like wrestlers!

Prince Crescendo held his reeling head, the sound of fighting ringing in his ears. He shook off the pain and dizziness, jumped to his feet, clutching his weapon, and gazed around for his steed.

"Pibcorn!" he shouted. "Pibcorn, come hither!"

A silvery-green deer with golden lyre-antlers reared and galloped up to Crescendo, who mounted him with a leap. Drawing the reins in, he turned Pibcorn around and charged into the raging conflict.

Prince Andante rushed forward, playing his instrument loudly and splendidly and the Discords found it impossible to prevent his onslaught. Covering their hearing holes, they fell to the ground, senseless, their helmets and grotesque masks unable to protect them. He saved three trapped Concords and then rushed on.

"So, ya powerful, eh, lick-spittle!" a grinding voice growled and a big Discord, all in sickly yellow, with a leering, lecherous mask, rode noisily in front of Prince Andante. Two large black discs were in the Discord's hands.

"Ya won't better the great Baron Grae Ting!" he snarled menacingly. Before Andante could use his music-maker, Grae Ting crashed the metal discs together and Andante's instrument broke into a thousand tinkling pieces. Stunned, he was dragged from his mount by five Discords who shattered his eardrums.

Crescendo saw this and charged at Baron Grae Ting singing wildly for revenge. Before the Discord had time to crash his discs together, Crescendo produced such a high-pitched note that Grae Ting's head burst like a water-melon and he fell to the ground. The five other Discords who had done away with Prince Andante then charged Crescendo. But five Concords led by Prince Andante's young son, De Capo, Captain of the Concords, lunged forward. Captain De Capo hastily dispatched the Noise-makers. Crescendo, deeply saddened by Prince Andante's loss, turned his steed about and plunged into another part of the fray.

The battle was fiercer than ever. At one moment, Music seemed to be gaining, the next Noise surged louder – and all the time, both Concords and Discords were losing their comrades.

Loud Crashbang was locked in confrontation with Prince Staccato. The grim Noise leader kept up a heavy assault on the Prince as he made frightful crashes and bangs with his Din-maker. The Prince countered the attacks with bursts of pure musical tone. Their mounts' teeth and antlers smashed and clashed in the frenzy of battle.

Prince Allegro was in combat with three Discords who were crashing their weapons in his ears. When Baron Dis Onance clashed up behind him on his hissing steed, he seemed doomed to be overcome. Prince Crescendo was fighting Clank Clapper – a Discord Captain of fearful stature – who was armed with a long, black jagged blade which created a head-spinning, mind-bursting racket.

With his violin weapon in hand, Crescendo started playing the most powerful tune that he had ever attempted. When the whirring noise increased from Clank Clapper's weapon, the music mounted from Prince Crescendo's violin. The ravelled air between the two, tormented by conflict, vibrated uncontrollably. Then, Prince Crescendo saw the weakening Prince Allegro. Like a Concord possessed, he played and the music that gushed forth from his violin, aimed at the Discord, was the most beautiful he had ever created.

Clank Clapper did not agree with this definition of beauty – his punctured head cracked into nineteen noisy pieces.

Prince Crescendo sped to Allegro, who was battling to stay mounted. Together they fought off their foes and gallantly surged forward into other conflicts.

In the darkening skies, the sound of Harmony clashing with Din could be heard by Sim Parth-Hee still searching for the answers to all he was seeking; including the answer to how everyone can understand each other and live in comfort with all – an answer he may never find, yet he will always search and be ready to help a good cause. The horrific sounds of battlers could also be heard by Vina performing her melancholy dance and longing for release and by the Jammings in Jazz.

Beneath the banks of the fast-flowing Acoustic, the drooling Rubats licked their lips.

*Ten thousand glittering instruments were
unsheathed and held high.*

15

Brother Darkness : Brother Light

"Do precisely what I say!" Conn Ductor commanded. "Put these around your heads!" With hands that moved quickly as liquid down a slope, he gave Melody and Tristan each a silvery-blue band. Tristan glanced at the band, then gazed at Conn Ductor with many questions in his eyes.

"But tell me..." began the boy.

The old Waltz Lord placed a reassuring hand on Tristan's left shoulder.

Tristan thought he was going to say something but he didn't. The chance to talk passed as a frightful cry tore through the sky. The children jumped. Conn Ductor looked sternly up and even Queen Rhapsody seemed startled by the terrible sound.

"Quickly, you two! Back inside!" urged Conn Ductor, in a voice that would stand no hesitations. "Put the protector bands around your head now!"

Hand in trembling hand, the two rushed inside behind the great bell doors and watched the mile-off danger draw ever nearer.

As the sky grew darker, thunderous flashes made the oncoming gloom blacker rather than lighter. Noise strangled the air. Melody and Tristan covered their ears with the protector bands Conn Ductor gave them. Despite this, they could hear the great 'Boom, boom, booming' that had commenced, filling every nook and cranny of sound like some monstrous out-of-time drum being beaten. Beaten. Beaten until Tristan's head ached as badly as it had when he had been a prisoner in Mr. Lampeter's 'Home Sweet Home.'

Tristan raised his eyes fearfully upwards. There, charging towards the Avenue of Statues, was a huge black chariot drawn by six enormous vulture-like creatures of green fire. A gigantic dark form with no visible features on its face except that above one great dark shoulder there hovered a blazing green Eye was riding in the chariot. The Eye had grown greatly since Tristan had seen it last.

By wearing the bands, neither Tristan nor Melody were able to hear the Sound Reaper's coming. Even so, they were wide-eyed with fear. The Chariot halted its forward flight and, with flashing lightning and a thunderous 'WHOOSH,' it spiraled to the ground.

With an upraised arm, Conn Ductor shielded his eyes from the glare. As soon as the chariot touched the ground, it burst into livid green flames with an earth-exploding 'BOOM!' shaking Queen Rhapsody so that she clutched onto the sides of her throne for support. Although wind-blown by the blast, Conn Ductor stood firm, his garment billowing backward.

Surrounded by angry, dancing green flames, the dark form towered thirty feet high before him. The blazing green Eye hovered menacingly above it.

"So, at last, you have come to me!" Conn Ductor said in a steady voice. As he stood in the gigantic shadow of the Sound Reaper, he appeared like a young sapling; straight, but frail, against the huge black sky. The odds seemed so loaded against him.

'How can anyone fight such a creature?' Tristan thought. He was so much more powerful than he had been

120

before. Only the Metronome seemed to trouble him slightly. Even so, when the huge dark form moved, the ground shook as at the beginning of some earthquake and the blackened air vibrated.

'I hope he doesn't remember how I tricked him,' thought Tristan, terrified. He fingered his tape recorder. Saying "Cacophony" aloud would have no effect now! Melody realised what he was thinking and gave him a 'go-ahead-and-return-I-won't-hold-it-against-you' look. But Tristan gave her a smile. There was no way that he was going to leave his friends now.

"GIVE UP, WALTZ LORD!" screamed the Sound Reaper, with ghastly loudness.

"Give up?" Conn Ductor responded in a goading fashion. "I know you now, evil one. It is you who has lost already."

Cacophony gave out an earth-shattering laugh and cries of anguish were heard from nearby Concord dwellings that were damaged by blasts of green fire from the Eye. Floating, it glowed blindingly, totally activated with wicked intent. The dark heavens filled with black fire clouds that rained down flames, searing the skies with sizzling sound.

Conn Ductor moved with swift purpose, waving his hands in magical motion, weaving musical patterns with the air. The flickering flame shower turned to harmless red rain that the ground soaked up.

Cacophony cursed. The hovering Eye blazed even brighter than before and began speeding about like a hound rushing up a scent. It laid waste all in its frenzied way, putting an end to seven young Concords who had hidden behind some bell trees.

Soon, the Sound Reaper was surrounded by a circle of broken statues and petrified lyre bushes and music trees. Where once had risen a Bell Grove, there tottered shadowy ruins made ghostly under the influence of the livid green

121

flames; like lop-sided skeletons of the dead.

With fire played menacingly about his hand, the huge dark form pointed a threatening black finger at Conn Ductor. "KNOW THIS – SO SHALL I DESTROY YOU WALTZ LORD AND ALL YOU SO VAINLY PROTECT!"

The Eye returned to linger malevolently above Cacophony's right shoulder. "FEEL MY POWER AND DESPAIR!"

Tristan felt faint at the terrible sound of his voices.

Conn Ductor stared up at the monster. "You shall soon be known as you are, Cacophony. Or shall I say, Obi Aleatoree. You don't have power, it has you."

Cacophony roared with rage at the Waltz Lord's words. They triggered true anger and a frightful thing occurred – the evil one began to change. Where his dark form had been, a hideous creature thrust a full sixty to seventy feet into the sky and stretched up like a giant four-headed lizard standing on its gigantic bulging rear legs. Huge claws were at the end of its raised arms. A pair of gargantuan green-veined wings flapped and clanged behind its back. In the middle of its four hideous mouths were the jaws of a demon shark. Bloodshot yellow flames flickered all over its slimy scaly green skin. The noise from it grew louder and louder. It was unbearable.

Melody gave Tristan an anxious look. Tristan attempted to put on a brave face but it took all his resolve to not lose consciousness.

The creature's four heads reared themselves, belching out great flames of fire at Conn Ductor, who stood firmly, not showing the fear that he must have felt. As the searing flames gushed at him, he waved his hands in measured circles in the air, turning the dreadful fire to harmless light that vanished in the greyness of Cacophony's wrath. Conn Ductor was growing tired with the great effort he was exerting, yet, "You won't ever defeat me, wicked one. For I know you now! Remember the ancient brotherhood pact you thought to destroy and YOU feel despair!" he said breathlessly.

Tristan marvelled at the courage of the old Waltz Lord. It gave him strength to see such frailty face up to an irresistible force such as the Sound Reaper. Melody held her head up, though terror glinted in her eyes.

With a circling roar, the monster blasted a torrent of flame at Conn Ductor. He just managed to intercept the billow of fire but part of the Bell Palace's great wall burst asunder and the Garden paving was burnt to ashes as bell flowers shrivelled up like charred and crumpled paper.

Tristan felt giddy with strain and fear. Melody was also affected. She put a reassuring hand on Tristan's shoulder and she managed to whisper, "I'm sure it will all be alright."

As if to mock her words, the monster extended its immense claws and hurled a ripping blow at Conn Ductor, who was knocked almost senseless to the ground. Four gloating grins spread across the evil creatures four faces and the Eye sparkled with deep malevolence.

"That's right," gasped Conn Ductor, trying desperately to catch his breath and crawl over to rest against a purple bell. "I dare your master, the Eye, to come closer. Or is great Aleatoree, Eye of Obi, frightened of an old Waltz Lord?"

Cacophony laughed, fire belching from his fang-filled jaws and the evil Eye soared in for the end. Tristan and Melody clung onto each other, fearfully turning their faces.

They didn't notice Conn Ductor concentrating on the Eye's course but when it reached a certain position, with a quick motion, Conn Ductor lifted the purple Bell. Beneath it was a perfect replica of the Golden Metronome, though much smaller and made of clear crystal. As the beam from the Great Metronome hit its now revealed surface, it shone gold. It was as if it was brought alive by the diamond beam now visibly coming from the Gem Goddess. It was like a receiver picking up the transmitted power of its great golden brother in the left hand of Tranquility. Conn Ductor constructed it for just this purpose. A trap. The Eye of Obi was caught in the vibrant beam that shimmered so strongly between the two. The Eye was motionless, unable to move from the power of unleashed good.

In the blinding glow of Music's source, the Eye's green fire went out; its evil lid closing over its wicked Eye, its energy gone!

Cacophony gave out a terrible cry of pain and dismay and the Sound Reaper's disguise fell away like grease paint under over-heated arc lights. He shrank down from his dark form's height and his monstrous stature by degrees as his true self was finally revealed.

Tristan and Melody stared wide-eyed with surprise. The creature that now stood before them and Conn Ductor, as he rose to his feet, was almost a mirror image of Conn Ductor himself, yet somehow gone wickedly wrong. Comm Poser was bald like Conn Ductor, but his long flowing black-green moustaches that almost touched the floor were distinctly different from Conn Ductor's moustaches of silver-blue. The creature was angry and very shocked! He cast a grave, baleful glance at the trapped Eye and then gazed with great bad temper at Conn Ductor.

Conn Ductor shook his head sorrowfully with recognition, whilst slowly regaining his strength. "Comm Poser, my greedy brother!" he said. "The mystery of your vanishing is revealed at last. Always looking for something, never content, and this is what you have finally found – disgrace and defeat! How could you think to rule others when you could not rule yourself! You put an end to Inno Vator, our brother!"

Comm Poser's mouth twisted to a sneer, chewing a curse. "Yes, 'brother,' all those things you say I did, I did. But I have not finished! You may have taken away the Eye but I still have a Waltz Lord's power. You shall never defeat me!" His deep socketed eyes blazed suddenly with dark fire.

"Brother Darkness, brother Light," Melody said, as if entranced."

Brother Darkness : Brother Light

"The Eye of Obi that you found on your travelling, and which you used for evil power, has been your downfall," Conn Ductor said, frowning at the baleful Comm Poser. "Ever since you wandered to Chaos Desert you were doomed! You were always ambitious, that I knew, and when you found the ancient head of Obi holding the Eye, Aleatoree, buried beneath the swirling sands and plucked out that Eye, your fate was sealed. Trickery sometimes succeeds for a short time but soon, it only tricks itself. I always suspected there was something strange about the whole affair of the coming of Cacophony but could never fathom it out until now. The Manchild helped me find that missing clue!"

"The milksop!" Comm Poser spat the words out. "I'll even that score!"

A shiver ran coldly up Tristan's spine.

Suddenly, Conn Ductor's eyes blazed with white fire,

warning his brother to make no move. "The Eye cannot break from the harmonious unity of the Metronome's beam. Only pure Tranquility can defeat pure Chaos. The Eye's illusions of total power against others were against you also, brother, and now you are but a strutting shadow speaking echoes!"

"Said with all the bitterness of an old friend," Comm Poser mocked. "You are weak 'brother,' always were with your 'grand' dreams of a gaudy Utopia with Inno Vator – do-gooders doing harm! But the sun shall set without your assistance. If you want peace, you'll have to die for it!"

And, with a violent wave of his hands, Comm Poser sent a shimmering ball of black fire and discordant sound spreading towards Conn Ductor, who, with a wave of his hands, sent it hurtling up harmlessly into the clearing sky where it exploded like a thousand dark fireworks.

Comm Poser glared at his brother, then, turning suddenly, defending himself always by attacking, he sent a black noise-ball sizzling fiercely towards Queen Rhapsody, who still sat beneath the statue of the Gem Goddess.

"Mother!" cried Melody in great alarm. But Conn Ductor gave out a single sustained musical note and the noise-ball transformed into falling bell-blossoms that landed softly as snowflakes at Queen Rhapsody's feet.

"SO!" Comm Poser boomed, then he fell from the top of his voice to the depths of silence.

Slowly and thoughtfully, he turned once more to Conn Ductor. The black fire in his eyes died down to a smoulder in the recesses of his deep socketed gaze. "Listen, brother," he began in a quiet, restrained voice, "be reasonable. We are the last of the Guardian Waltz Lords. Join forces with me. Release the Eye and we shall rule two Spheres. Think what good you will be able to perform with complete control over everyone! No one would dare be wicked or you would punish them terribly. Our Palace tops would pierce all skies; our banners fling out the winds from the greatest heights in both Audia and Lumio." He paused and looked at his brother with persuasive, pleading eyes, veiling his face with a smile. "All I want is…."

"Power for power's sake! I see it as easily as the Fugue flies, as clearly as a lake reflects!" said Conn Ductor harshly. "Don't bandy words. It is over, brother. You have lost!"

Comm Poser snarled, black fire leaping once more to the forefront of his malicious eyes. "Never!" he screamed and, in a black flash, was gone!

Comm Poser snarled, black fire leaping once more to the forefront of his malicious eyes. "Never!" he screamed.

16

A Drunken Weapon
Just Above Our Heads

"Where did he go?" Tristan asked, rushing to an awkward halt on one leg at Conn Ductor's side. Melody followed.

"Comm Poser, the traveller still has the secret of journeying to Lumio. That, I fear, is where he has gone," Conn Ductor sighed.

"Not again!"

"I should have stopped him!" Conn Ductor said, pulling with agitation on one side of his long silvery-blue moustache. "But, he is still powerful and I was weakened a great deal by the struggle with the evil Eye Aleatoree."

"You called him 'brother'?" asked Queen Rhapsody, who now approached.

"Yes, your Tranquil Majesty," Conn Ductor replied with a sad smile. "Comm Poser was one of the Waltz Lords. No good man ever grew powerful all at once. When he gained the Eye, his pure name was lost and he became Cacophony. Even now that he has been restored to his former self, all good that was once so much part of him has been perverted. He has been paid with his own coins of hate and greed!"

Tristan still perceived traces of white fire smouldering in the depth of Conn Ductor's knowing eyes.

"You have done so much for us, Manchild," Conn

Ductor began, with a trace of hesitation in his voice. "I must now ask you to do more!" I cannot journey to Lumio. If we are to finally overcome the lingering evil of Cacophony, you must return to your Sphere and find him."

"Tell me the worst!" Tristan said, smiling ruefully.

Melody looked apprehensively at the new danger that faced the Manchild.

"He no longer has the power of the Eye and therefore cannot cast illusions or change shape." Conn Ductor stroked his long thin chin. "In your Sphere, he will seem the same as here."

"But how will I find him, Conn Ductor?"

"We must go to Bop Shoowah's Tower of Mod together, you and I," Conn Ductor said.

Tristan felt a pang of happiness. 'Perhaps Scherzo would still be there!' He would do anything to see the little fellow again.

"Until Cacophony is captured, he will be a raised and dangerous weapon forever lingering above all our heads," said Queen Rhapsody.

"A drunken weapon at that." Tristan recalled how his father muttered on about drivers who drank too much. 'Drunken weapons aimed at us,' he called them.

"I want to go with you," Melody said firmly. "I am as strong and courageous as any Concord – nothing can frighten me now."

"I know, but that cannot be Princess," said Conn Ductor seriously.

"Why not?" she began, more firmly still.

"Be calm, my daughter," Queen Rhapsody interrupted with gentle strength. "I need you with all your courage here. There is much to do."

There was a pause. Then, "Alright, Mother," Melody conceded, putting a happy face over her feelings of disappointment. Tristan, too, felt disappointed to be leaving

Melody but he knew what he must do.

"Come with me, Manchild!" Conn Ductor said. "We must be swift!"

"Music be with you, Manchild," Queen Rhapsody said.

"Goodbye!" Melody added sadly. "Come back soon!" She kissed Tristan on the cheek and hugged him quickly. Tristan smiled, hugging her back; then he followed Conn Ductor into the damaged Bell Palace.

"How are we going to reach Pop quickly?" Tristan thought with discomfort at the prospect of the long journey ahead, remembering the lengthy and eventful trek with Scherzo.

"Manchild, Manchild, you underestimate me!" said the Waltz Lord. "Now that my powers are returned by the Metronome, even though I may not be able to travel to Lumio, still I can go anywhere in Audia."

Conn Ductor led Tristan into, "My journey room!" he said proudly, "I created it myself years ago!"

"Very impressive!"

As they entered the square room, there was a huge relief map showing different areas of Audia on the wall facing them. In each area, there was a Sphere of a particular colour. On another wall, a rack held a series of long transparent rods.

"Take hold of my hand, Manchild," Conn Ductor said, taking one of the rods from its place in the rack. "Now you will see how simple travelling can be!"

"That'll be a change!" smiled Tristan quietly.

The old Concord raised the transparent rod and, with the end, touched an orange Sphere in the centre of the area clearly labelled 'POP – Cit. Amp Mountains – Re. MOD.' Immediately, the Sphere began to glow and the transparent rod became orange. There was a low musical humming and everything began to fade.

In a moment, they were standing in the courtyard of Bop Shoowah's Tower of Mod. A section of the high red wall had been completely burnt and demolished. There was now a pile of rubble where Bunkum and Bosh's house had once been. One of the great silver gates of the main entrance was unhinged and swung disjointedly, like a dangling puppet with half its strings cut.

At the top of the high tower, a large hole yawned mockingly where Cacophony had entered. There was an unnerving woebegone feeling to the place, like a town after sudden catastrophe.

"Scherzo!" Tristan was unable to contain himself any longer. "Scherzo, are you here?"

"Take care, Manchild," Conn Ductor cautioned. "One can't be certain who or what to expect in circumstances such as these."

Tristan stopped, statue-like. Something moved just to the front and right, crunching behind some fallen broken stones.

"Show yourself, be you friend or foe!" the old Waltz Lord commanded firmly. "Know I am Conn Ductor, Waltz Lord of Harmony!"

There was a loud sigh of relief along with the noise of rubble moving as a large figure, like a lumbering goods train, came chugging out into the open.

"It's Bosh, one of the Bop Shoowah's giants!" said Tristan happily.

"Where is your master?" Conn Ductor asked in a clear, strong voice.

The giant smiled amiably and pointed a large awkward finger at Mod.

Conn Ductor gave a friendly nod. "Come," he told Bosh. "Lead the way!" And the two followed the Giant into the ramshackle tower.

The hall was dirty, with a stormy downpour of dust that had settled into a sheet of off-white, covering everything. If it had been a person, it would have had its head in its hands. It looked so miserable. The fire that had once invited Tristan and Scherzo in after their long journey was now but a memory – a ghost that had been laid too long.

They followed the trundling Bosh to the winding stairs. The Giant then pointed up the stairs and wandered off. Up and up the two wound until, "Oh dear, when it's ended, it's only just begun. So much to be made right and good. Still, to endure what is unendurable is true endurance!"

"Bop Shoowah!" cried Tristan with elation to Conn Ductor. Tristan was about to call 'Scherzo' when....

"Yes, a sound I also did distinctly hear, from a voice that I know to be wonderfully familiar."

Tristan heard this and with bounding joy, shouted, "Scherzo!" happily. Sure enough, a little figure scurried out of a chamber and down the stairs, hair changing wildly.

"Oh, life on me has smiled, once again I see the good Manchild!" chirped Scherzo, merrily grabbing hold of Tristan and giving him an enormous hug that quite knocked the breath out of the boy.

Conn Ductor smiled. "It is good to see you safe and well, old friend," he said.

"It is the gladdest sight to see, never again shall I be unhappy!" Scherzo's hair turned luminous corn flower blue with peacock red polka dots as he shook the Waltz Lord's hand. There was a 'Yeah, Yeah' bark and the bee-winged dog came buzzing in a spiral to a halt upside-down just above Tristan's head, giving him a slurpy backward lick with his long purple tongue. Close behind, there scuttled down the stairs, the tall and remarkable figure of Bop Shoowah. "Well, well. How life turns up silver linings one upon another!" He clapped his long, thin hands together. "Unexpected meetings are always the most pleasing!"

"Bop Shoowah..." Conn Ductor began.

"You must try some of my peppered chops whilst you're here – sounds splendid, eh? My kitchens are not too damaged and Bunkum is quite extraordinary at cooking peppered chops. I have not had so many guests for simply ages – to eat alone kills the appetite."

"Bop Shoowah!" Conn Ductor said in a firm voice that was friendly, yet not to be overruled. "This is no accident, but a planned meeting. I am glad to see you are well, though sorry the Sound Reaper caused so much damage to Mod."

"Yes." Bop Shoowah shook his head sadly.

"I have a favour to ask of you, Keeper of Pop, and the time is now," said Conn Ductor with firm insistence. "The battle still rages in the Baroque Plains through this oncoming lapse-light and the outcome is uncertain. I have defeated Cacophony in Harmony."

"Defeated the Sound Reaper! Well, roast eggs! My Lady Electrika would have been pleased!" Bop Shoowah exclaimed.

"Dust becomes dawn freshly begun, and ashes flames of a newly born sun!" Scherzo proclaimed merrily.

"Rejoice a little," said Conn Ductor, not rejoicing at all, "but in another form, he has gone to Lumio to seek vengeance. We must capture him!"

"Oh, you want to use the Moog! I shouldn't rely on that if I were you. It is badly damaged, totally defunk I think. My Lady Electrika would have been most upset. Not that I ever used it, you understand. Never had any interest in Lumio, too busy here!"

Conn Ductor frowned. "Still," he said, "Bop Shoowah, would you be so kind as to direct us to where it is kept?"

"Of course. If you swallow your pen, use a pencil I always say." The worthy fellow munched a nut. "The measure of a man is not what he achieves but what he wants to achieve."

"Even so, even so!" Conn Ductor replied.

They followed Bop Shoowah up the winding piano-key stairway that became more cracked as they approached the torn wall Cacophony had entered through. Finally, they reached the high hall where the Moog Room lay.

"What a state!" Tristan exclaimed, looking at the cracks and holes. A dark breeze lifted his hair and seemed to whisper the sounds of distant battle windily in his ear.

"Wherever the evil one comes in, all he leaves is ruin!" said Scherzo, his hair turning pea-green with pink stars.

"Yeah, Yeah," yapped Yeah, Yeah, landing at Bop Shoowah's feet.

They followed the Keeper of Pop into the Moog Room. "Alas, things are not what they once were." He sighed, pointing an outstretched hand to the Moog Ring on the floor, seemingly drained of all energy and covered with dust and fallen stones.

"Now what?" Tristan asked.

Conn Ductor strode purposefully up to the fallen ring and touched its surface with searching fingers, clearing it of rubble.

"It still vibrates," he said. "There is still some power left. If I can boost this, then it may work once more. Scherzo, old friend, take this!" Conn Ductor gave the little Concord his Journey Rod. Scherzo's hair turned orange.

Conn Ductor then placed both hands on the Ring and gave out a low prolonged musical hum. Soon, the circular keyboard began to rise. "Quickly, Manchild!" commanded the old Waltz Lord. "Step in!"

Tristan did. Immediately, the Ring lowered itself around him. Bop Shoowah looked amazed.

"You know what to do, my boy?" Conn Ductor asked.

Tristan nodded and began to play the keys. Soon, the notes changed from high and distant to low and near. Then, the vision balloon appeared. "I wish to find Cacophony," Tristan said with slow clarity.

A scene grew, filling the balloon. He peered at it intensely. "He's in Four Seasons Park in my home town," he

135

gasped.

In the scene, a dirty tramp-like man was wandering between high bushes chanting some strange curses. There was no mistaking the dark fire that smouldered in the hate-filled depths of his jackal eyes. Then, the image slowly drained away. The Moog Ring fell once more to the dusty floor.

"Why has he gone back to my town?" Tristan feared the worst.

The worst was realised. "Revenge, I fear," said Conn Ductor. "He is summoning all his knowledge of old, working his way round your town to spread a net of power. When he is ready, he will pull it in!"

"What must I do?" Tristan asked, anxiously. "Tell me!"

"You must return to your Sphere now and make him leave before he does any harm."

"By saying his name?" Tristan asked, eager with worry.

"No, Manchild. I fear that without Obi Aleatoree's power and burden, he would simply keep returning. We must make his capture permanent." Conn Ductor held up four golden bells attached to a silver disc. "This will stick to anything that is out of harmony and start a ringing that will drain all chaos into music. Comm Poser will not be able to stand the pure sound and, as his power is confiscated, he will have to return to Audia."

"Sounds difficult, as usual!" Tristan gazed thoughtfully at the golden bells of the silver disc, "And dangerous!"

"It is," said Conn Ductor, plainly. "And you must return now! As always, time runs out. I will see you arrive in the Park. You will not be alone. You never have been."

"O.K." Tristan took the disc.

Scherzo looked sad, his hair turned deep blue.

"Do not forget, there is nothing to fear except fear itself," said Bop Shoowah. "The fly that doesn't want to be swatted is most secure landing on the fly-swatter." He waved a reassuring finger in the air.

"Goodbye, good luck, make a winning tune, and never forget to come back soon!" Scherzo wiped a rainbow tear from his dumpy red cheek.

"Don't worry. I will!" said Tristan, turning the magic tape over.

"Take care, Manchild!" said Conn Ductor. "May the Music be within you always!"

"It is not what we do but the spirit in which we do it that is important and as I ...." began Bop Shoowah, suddenly forgetting what he was going to say in a pang of sadness. So, he just passed the boy a handful of nuts and gave him a pat on the back.

"Yeah, Yeah," barked Yeah Yeah and did three little spins upside-down in the air especially for Tristan. Tristan turned on the tape player.

The tune began and the scene of waving hands started to fade away.

Tristan heard Scherzo saying things that were rather jumbled, except for the word, "Tristan."

"You said my name!" exclaimed the boy – but they could no longer hear him.

The tall and remarkable figure of Bop Shoowah
was accompanied by Yeah Yeah.
"Well, well. How life turns up silver
linings one upon another!"

17

The Final Tolling :
A Confused Climax

With a rapid survey of the immediate area, Tristan started a cautiously methodical walk around the familiar grounds of Four Seasons Park; now so strangely silent and disquieting. Even the old boat keeper was nowhere to be seen.

He couldn't find the evil Comm Poser anywhere and began to worry that he was too late. He quickened his pace. Then, he threw himself behind a large lilac bush. He caught a glimpse of the bent back of a dirty-grey coat disappearing behind a clump of pines near the Park's North gate not more than a hundred yards away.

"That's him for sure!" Tristan was sweating with apprehension.

Comm Poser slipped out of the side gate like a viper and slid down the road on his poisonous path. Tristan followed as secretly as he could, catching every breath he breathed to prevent any excess sound that might betray him. Worry, like an ingrowing toenail, nagged at each step he took.

Whenever Comm Poser slowed down, Tristan ducked behind a parked car or hopped agily behind a suburban wall. Soon, it became clear that Comm Poser was travelling in a definite, all-too-familiar direction.

'What terrible evil is he planning once he reaches his

destination?' Tristan wondered anxiously as he followed on the trail that he instinctively knew would lead to Mr. Lampeter's house.

Then, Comm Poser suddenly stopped completely still. Tristan dived headfirst behind a parked Mini-Metro on December Drive. As soon as he landed he grazed his right knee painfully and broke out in a cold nervous tremble. He craned his neck and peered at the figure standing motionless, a whip-stroke away. Comm Poser turned his head slowly round, like a cobra sensing prey. Just out of view, Tristan gazed fearfully; transfixed by the glimpse of eyes that burnt deeply with smouldering black hate.

'Should I throw the disc at him now?' Tristan asked himself.

The decision was made for him. The evil one suddenly averted his stare and continued on his course.

A little further on, after Comm Poser slinked darkly into Mid-Summer Mews, he stopped once more. Tristan, his heart thumping wildly, jumped over a nearby garden wall and crouched breathlessly behind the wall. Comm Poser turned round like a wolf on its trapped victim. Tristan just caught a glimpse of the dark flames dancing from his black eyes.

The wicked one waived his right hand in the glittering air. With a throwing motion and malicious laugh, he sent a thin stream of dark fire. A sizzling noise plowed through the air, shooting towards the horrified boy.

Only by a hair's breadth did Tristan manage to jump back as the brick wall in front of him split into smouldering ruins. All the grass around him withered and died.

"So!" Comm Poser smirked, "I thought as much! Interfering becomes a habit, eh? I wondered how long it would take for *you* to arrive!"

'This is it!' Tristan decided. 'I'm well and truly done for!' He was too far away to throw the Bell Disc.

"Cheer up - the worst is yet to come!" Comm Poser

mocked, starting to circle his hands once more in the air, the buzzing static ravelling the atoms. In an instant, the buzzing changed to a sizzling rasping sound as particles of quiet air were forced into noisy fire…..

…. "Then I said, 'Listen, mate, if your band can play better than the Ramones, I'll be a football manager and drink water beds!' Hey, you know, I feel really tired!"

"Yeah. Same here. Anyway, then what did ol' Spikey Jim say, Chaz?" The conversation came from three cyberpunks suddenly appearing from out of the house just next to Tristan, who still stood pressed against the wall.

"Well…." began Chaz, but he never finished. The noise-bolt meant for Tristan hit him full on. His two friends froze in disbelief. Their smitten companion turned into smouldering black fire that began a crazy nightmare dance and then shot comet-like into the sky, exploding in a bright shower of sparkling ashes. Both youths looked up at the dust falling and then, with tears in their eyes, collapsed. Tristan jumped into the house from which they had come.

Comm Poser cursed loudly and bounded like a jackal around the corner and away. Tristan emerged to follow him when, "What the deuce has been doing here?" a portly man wearing khaki shorts said. He was busy polishing some regimental medals as he marched out of his front door.

"Nothing!" Tristan said, anxiously gazing to see if he could find Comm Poser.

"Nothing! I saw the fire!" The man moved threateningly forward on gorgonzola veined legs pointing at the two prostrate figures and then up to some ash that was still falling.

"Nothing! Blithering nonsense!" His voice filled with indignant wrath. "I know what you mean, heard it all before!" His fat, wobbling face turned scarlet. His military moustache stood at attention and bristled accusingly with emotion as he propped himself against what remained of the broken, blackened wall. He looked almost as if he had been eating

141

firecrackers all day and was set to explode. For some reason, he started gasping for air. "Enemies! Enemies everywhere! Invaders, invaders, a pocket full of H bombs, a fission a fission, we all fall....down!" And, yawning, uncontrollably, he suddenly lost consciousness and joined the two other fallen figures on the ground.

Weariness started to fill Tristan too. So, shaking his head, he took off as fast as his feet would carry him after Comm Poser. The nearer he drew to Mr. Lampeter's house, the more powerful he became. Fear grew tangible, clinging like glue to his face and hands.

The sky was becoming increasingly overcast, although it was mid-day. There was a tingling tiredness in the air, as if in conspiracy. Then, with horror, Tristan saw several people slumped, sleeping on the pavement by the bus shelter. A little further on, he ran past a Bedford van and Mazda hatchback that had crashed because their drivers had fallen asleep – and still were! One seemed quite badly injured but there was nothing Tristan could do except to keep on.

Tristan stood at the edge of Winter Walk, staring at the teacher's 'Home Sweet Home.' Everything was wrong. There wasn't a person in evidence anywhere who wasn't sleeping. Comm Poser was mounting the steps slowly, one by one.

'A reason for everything and everything for a reason,' Bop Shoowah had said once. Comm Poser was returning to the place in Lumio where he felt strongest.

'Traces of the evil Eye's power might still be remaining there!' Tristan sweat, dread mounting. Comm Poser's hand was on Lampeter's front door. Tristan had to act quickly. He ran at full speed towards the demented Waltz Lord who turned as rapidly as a rattlesnake, stopping the boy with a fiery glare.

"Ha, ha!" he laughed with lingering bad intent. His baleful eyes blazed like dark furnaces. He leered with a grimace that Tristan thought the devil himself would have been proud of. Comm Poser threw off his grimy overcoat, revealing the greeny-black cassock. A chain of green eyes was about his middle. His dark cloak, like bats' wings, billowed in the disturbed and mounting wind.

"You shall be the first to pay my price, scum!" he cried. "But first know that you will not be the last. I have set lines of force all round this town. All people within are now asleep. Using all my energies, I shall draw my power together and they shall wake under *my* control. Then, through time, I shall grow and, using every atom of power, I shall die; becoming a spirit spreading my influence until I can cause government to war against government. Yes, World War Three! Your race, already aggressive to each other, will be primed to destroy itself without thought. It won't take much to set the whole thing off! Ha ha! Total destruction of all life on this accursed Sphere! Think of the glorious chaos and nuclear noise! A truly beautiful idea is it not?"

"No!" Tristan gasped. "You're mad!"

"Mad! Ha! Come, say the bogey man. I have brought you a nightmare fit to ride" Comm Poser gloated horribly as he made a motion with his bony claw-like hands, setting the air about him on fire. Tristan could hardly bear the crackling, mounting noise. He felt weak and incredibly tired. His strength was being sucked away! Mr. Lampeter's prize roses began to shrivel and die, his paving stones cracked, and the grass and trees singed. Everything was being consumed in sizzling flames.

It was Tristan's very last chance. Gathering the ebbs of his energy, he threw the Bell Disc at Comm Poser. With a musical 'THUMP!' it struck and stuck on his chest.

"Ahhh!" he cried terribly, stricken with sudden pain. A bolt he had aimed at Tristan shot up like a harmless football into the sky, bursting into a dark fountain. The noise it created was drowned out by the tinkling bells. Each scream and movement caused the Bells to toll and weaken the deranged

Waltz Lord.

"What have you done, Milksap?" he cried. "What have you done?" With a final crackle, the flames in the air disappeared. Comm Poser stood motionless. Tristan edged slightly closer, tiredness gradually left him.

"I have done what Conn Ductor said I must!" the boy said firmly.

"Curse him and curse you!" The flames that flickered in his deep-socketed eyes suddenly died down to a dusky smouldering. His voice changed, becoming pleasant. "Look, good Manchild!" he urged softly, "I wasn't really going to harm anyone. I haven't the power. It is just my way! I should have explained that all I wanted was an item I left here."

"You had no right to set that man on fire!" Tristan said.

"Not my fault if the little fool was in the way," he bitterly spurted out.

"The greatest of faults is to be conscious of none!" Tristan retorted adamantly.

Comm Posor coughed painfully. "Anyone can make a mistake," he pleaded.

"Yes, but only a fool continues in it." Tristan felt strong and resolute.

"I meant no harm to anyone," Comm Posor insisted. "Those that once sought my help now seek my downfall. It was the wicked Eye of Obi that changed me. But, Conn Ductor is wrong. I am Comm Posor once more - Guardian Traveller of the Spheres! I simply wish to be myself. Please, good 'Tristan,' take these Bells from me."

Calling Tristan by his name and talking in such persuasive tones caught the boy rather off guard. He became indecisive as to what was completely right and wrong. His thoughts faltered.

"Please take these Bells off me, good 'Tristan,'" Comm Posor said gently. "And we shall be such good friends. I reward my friends well. I will make you Lord of Lumio. You shall want for nothing. Think of the glory and power for one so noble and wise as yourself!"

Tristan listened. He had learnt much in the last few days and he knew that it was the old Cacophony talking. Comm Posor was but a name for the evil that was still the Sound Reaper. "Never!" Tristan said, moving a few paces back. "Evil one!"

Comm Posor glared at him – the hatred and wrath that filled him began seeping to the surface once more. His thin lips curled into a curse. "So!" he spat the words out – his whole face shining with a dark red glow that made Tristan think of the way embers shine under the dull coals of a dying fire about to spark up fiercely one more time before the fire goes out for good.

The Bells tolled his time away as Comm Posor was in great distress and vainly writhed to free himself. Then, he fixed Tristan in his stare and, with an incredible summoning of wicked will, he ran and leapt on the boy like a panther on its prey.

One long-nailed hand grabbed hold of Tristan's neck. The other rose viciously to land a thudding, destructive blow that smashed into Tristan's face.

"No, Comm Posor – Cacophony!" screamed the boy over and over and over again to the sound of the jangling, ringing, tolling bells.

Tristan felt a violent tug, something snapped, and a dreadful blackness like death gushed over and into him.

The sky was becoming increasingly overcast,
although it was mid-day.
There was a tingling tiredness in the air, as if in conspiracy.

18

Tristan Solo Once Again

"Where am I?" Tristan asked slowly.

"You're in my study, Laddie! Shipshape and Bristol fashion," replied a friendly, squeaking voice. "I found you outside my doorstep. Quite unconscious you were. Something curious had happened. A fire or the like; had a nasty fall, did you!"

"Cacophony – Comm Posor," Tristan mumbled to himself, trying to remember exactly what had happened. He gazed at the bindings of the books that lined the wall. They were like clenched mouths refusing to open to explain or comfort. In his head, 'It was a dark and stormy night,' repeated itself over and over again.

"I've phoned your father. He's coming over right away! You know, Smith, you've caused rather a stir. You've been missing for nigh on thirty-six hours. This will never do, you'll have to explain a few things, Laddie!" His voice had become the teacher's tone that Tristan knew so well.

Then, Tristan suddenly looked round in a near frenzy. He searched himself and where he was lying.

"My tape recorder!" he said frantically. "Did you see one outside?"

"Now relax, Smith. You've been through a lot of strain," said 'Moley' Lampeter.

147

'He doesn't know the half of it!' thought Tristan, springing to his feet before either of the Lampeter's could do a thing and rushed out into the street.

He searched everywhere; under the charred bushes, between the cracked stones, on the pavement, up and down the street. Nothing! Absolutely nothing! Comm Posor had performed one last malicious act before he had been forced home – the wicked one had grabbed Tristan's recorder and taken it with him.

"Evil, evil creature," Tristan muttered, holding back frustrated fury. "Oh, if only I had known, I would never have said his foul name. How am I ever going to get back to Audia now?"

The next moment he felt arms wrapped around him....

They were his mother's. "Tristan, darling," she said happily.

"Hello, son!" The thankful odour wafted with friendship over to him as his father approached from out of the old Rover, smiling all over his face. Tristan thought to himself how he had foolishly forgotten how worried his parents must have been. But, then again, they would have been far more worried if they believed what he had been through - which he was sure they wouldn't.

"Hello!" Tristan said happily, forgetting his troubles for a while. He could see they were safe and that Comm Posor was unable to hurt them. All his experiences taught him to value and follow through with true feelings before they fade or were devalued.

"The wanderer returneth!" said Mr. Lampeter, coming out to meet them.

"Goodness, gracious, Mr. Lampeter, what has happened to your garden?" asked Tristan's mother, catching a first sight of the charred remains that were still strewn about the doorstep of his 'Home Sweet Home.'

"Well, dear Lady, I'm afraid that is rather a mystery,"

sighed Mr. Lampeter, taking off his round glasses and polishing them with an immaculately white handkerchief. "The last week has been most strange, most strange; what, with disappearing burglars and all."

Suddenly, "Tristy, have you something to do with this? Where have you been?" His mother's voice grew sterner, recalling how much commotion he had caused. Tristan tried to think as quickly as possible. There was no way he could tell them the truth. The less they knew, the less danger they would be in if any evil lingered from Cacophony. "I...I went to Four Seasons Park!" A bad excuse is better than none! "And, I watched the football match as I listened to music on my recorder. I must have fallen asleep because, when I woke, it was dark, very dark....and my tape player was gone. I've spent all this time searching - up until I tripped over and knocked myself out searching for it."

"Mean you've been away for thirty-six hours because you lost your tape recorder! Are you serious?" exclaimed his father, taking his pipe out of his mouth incredulously. "We've had the police looking for you. Still, you're safe and that's the main thing."

"Look, honestly, Dad. That is the truth," Tristan replied in the most honest voice that he could muster. In his mind, Tristan could hear Scherzo say:

A boy said he would die, before he would lie-
such was his love of the truth ...
and die he did - right in the prime of his youth!

"Thank goodness you're here and alright and...you've got a nerve!" complained his mother. "Your music will be the death of us all!"

'If only you knew,' Tristan thought. 'If only you knew!' And in his mind he thought he heard Conn Ductor whispering, 'Remember, Manchild, the humanity we all share is more important that the confusions we may not.'

Tristan heard Conn Ductor whispering,
'Remember, Manchild, the humanity we all share is more
important than the confusions we may not.'
And he thought about his friends so far away - so close to his heart.

19

More Things in Heaven and Earth

Two weeks; fourteen days; fourteen nights; three hundred and thirty-six hours; twenty thousand one hundred and sixty minutes – goodness knows how many seconds!

"No news from Audia," Tristan sighed. "Nothing!" All he could think was that even now, the Lords of Din might be rulers of Audia. Comm Posor escaped and may be restored to his full power as Cacophony with the evil Eye of Obi Aleatoree hovering above his right shoulder, preparing an invasion of Lumio. And what could he do? "It really is a nice, tidy mess!"

At the beginning of the third week, with no word from Audia, Tristan ached with heavy depression. Apprehension jittered through the air. The bitterest thing about today's sorrow is the memory of yesterday's joy. He couldn't cope and played truant from St. Julian's, going to his old retreat in Four Seasons Park beneath the big bush. Once again, the laburnum was coming into yellow bloom, yielding its golden sunlight and the green night of clematis leaves also proudly held its purple stars.

He watched and wondered and waited. Nothing ever came except the inevitable twilight as a crimson sunset shed its petals one by one. On silent feet, the shadows wandered into the Park, kicking the colours half-heartedly aside. This sad weariness mirrored exactly what Tristan felt as he got up, turned, and slowly walked away. He didn't notice the figure sitting in a boat outside the boat shed. He didn't notice the figure looking at him through piercing blue and slightly anxious eyes.

"Come here," the figure said. "Come here. Don't you hate it when someone answers their own questions? I do."

Tristan turned and saw the old boat keeper beckoning to him. He walked over.

"Sit down. I think I can help you. I've always kept an eye out for you, Music-Child." the old boat keeper said. "I want to tell you something."

He stared at Tristan with his piercing blue eyes. Silently, the boy sat in a boat beside him. "When I was a boy, about your age and a bit of a loner," the boat keeper began, "I had a small boat that I used to row on a little stream that ran past the bottom of my parents' garden. One day, a magician sent me two magic oars and two magic words. I knew I must close my eyes, put the magic oars into the water, say the magic words, and row. As I rowed, I moved effortlessly into Elsanador – a land full of magnificent streams that sang as I rowed. I saw diamonds sparkle on the banks of the streams and in the light red water. Everything was brightly coloured and all the Elsanadonians used boats to travel from place to place. These boats talked to other owners and to each other. These boats lived for their wood came from the mystical forest of Withymead. No one was ever lonely."

He paused a moment and then continued, "I was never lonely, for I fell in love with the magician's daughter. She was glorious and we would float past red and blue trees and orchid orchestras. It was a land of music. I watched the magicians perform such marvelous feats. Then, there came a day when one magician said that I must help him, for that was one purpose of bringing me to Elsanador. Something was creeping into the forest and killing the trees. This destruction was spreading. Many of the boats no longer talked or lived. They seemed like dead wood. And the magician knew and said, 'You can help them.' And help them I did and Vina marvelled at my new-found strength. But she was tricked by a spell cast from afar and she vanished from us."

He continued, "Then, the magician insisted that I must return home, for there I would need to keep watch and perhaps find a way to break the spell that was cast on Vina, for our world holds the key to so many others and I would become a Watcher and protector. I hoped to find the answer."

The old boat keeper paused again. Tristan gazed at him, transfixed, as he stroked a bonny boat beside him and said something to it that Tristan couldn't quite make out. Two ducks splashed about; ripples reflected their friendly exchange. Then, looking at the boy, he began again.

"Return I did. And, for the love of Vina and Elsanador, I keep watch. So, even though I am old, I am the Keeper who keeps watching and keeps hope with all. I know of your struggle and the world you protect. That is the thing – never lose hope. There are many forms of existence beyond us. As long as we believe in ourselves and the countless possibilities of life, then all the worlds without end will survive. Some may think me an idle old rascal, ha! I'm not. There is magic all around us and I'm just waiting, longing for it to come for me again. I am waiting for the time when I shall return to Vina and Elsanador and be made young again. He who longs the most, lives the longest. Not everyone is chosen by the Magic, but I know you have been, my boy. So, if you feel in the dark at the moment, remember, as light darkens, so sometimes darkness lightens."

The boat keeper continued, "We are all wrapped in each other's wishes. Music is the magic that fills the wand of your silence. Remember without your music, life would be a mistake and that is what the evil ones want - to make all life a

153

mistake that will be regretted forever. But the truth is music, pure and rising, is a higher revelation than all wisdom and philosophy."

He stopped, still staring at the boy.

"Is it true?" Tristan asked earnestly. "Is it true what you've said? Would you like to hear about Audia? About my world of magic? About...."

The boat keeper smiled a knowing bulldog smile and his blue eyes sparkled and Tristan fell silent.

"There is a fence with spaces you could look through if you wanted to. A tear - child who saw this thing one song-filled summer evening took out the spaces with great care and built a castle in the air. We are all searching for something. It is tiring in the end and then it is only the beginning," the boat keeper said and patted the boy on the back. "I am the Keeper of this world who keeps watch and I know that such as you and I are in the front line of the battle between good and evil in all its forms. But you have given me something I needed to complete my task – defeating Chaos has made an invisible door visible for me. I bless you, my boy. So, now, you too must keep watch and wait when you may be needed next."

Then, turning, he started talking to a boat again.

Tristan waited for a while, then got up. "Thank you," he said. But Tristan could see that the old boat keeper was engrossed in his conversation with the boat and so he walked home. His mind was full of what he had been told. Somehow, the boat keeper's words merged with those of Vina, the deathless. 'It is good that different ones meet from time to time. As long as such as you can feel for one such as me, then there is hope left for both of us,' is what she said. If Tristan could have seen the old boat keeper's face, he would have seen the wrinkles start to slowly fade. Now, some distant spell began to break and a magic door's lock clicked open for the old man to return to Elsanador.

"Yes," he said to himself. "I shan't lose hope. To have

had the chance to go to a Magic land in the first place is more than most people ever get. Yes, to have been there. To have been there. To have been."

And the moon opened like a fresh white rose in the night sky.

"Sit down. I think I can help you. I've always
kept an eye out for you, Music-Child,"
the old boat keeper said. "I want to tell you something."

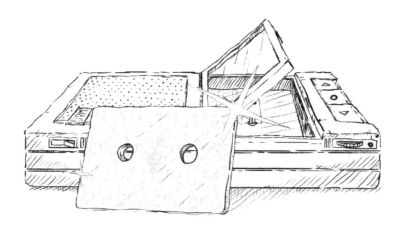

The Magic Tape Again

20

Hope's Refrain

"Where have you been?" His mother's voice quivered with impatience. "Do you realise what time it is?"

"Mr. Clayton rang." His father's voice was an accusation. "You've been missing class again!"

"I know," Tristan said. "I'm sorry I've been acting like a spoiled brat. I...I've just been feeling depressed lately. But I'll snap out of it. I promise," he clarified.

The sincerity in Tristan's voice placated his parent so much so that they returned to their normal and caring selves.

"Here, Tristan. Your father and I thought you might find this of use." And, smiling, she handed Tristan a new tape recorder.

"Oh, Mum, Dad, thanks ever so much," Tristan said, taking it. "It's fantastic!"

He gave both his parents a hug. "Thanks again. I don't deserve it." Then, after a cup of cocoa, he went to bed.

He lay awake and mused, 'If Din had won, surely something would have happened by now. Surely! But then again, who can really tell or be sure of anything?'

As Tristan was thinking such troubled thoughts, he fell into a troubled sleep where a huge green eye set fire to everything around him, and he and Melody and Scherzo were trapped in a cage....and the flames were getting nearer and nearer....

Suddenly, a bell rang – a sound that seemed a world away. Was it a dream?

Perhaps at first, but then certainly not. For Tristan woke and the ringing continued, moving closer. He jumped from his bed. On his table was a tape – not golden this time, but of the purest crystal he had ever seen. Tristan's heart thumped for hope and joy! Hurriedly, he dressed. With anticipating fingers, he slipped the tape into his recorder and switched the player on. He waited for the music and the fading as his journey began, but... no music! No fading!

He quietly sat down on the edge of his bed, deeply disappointed. Then, he heard a voice coming not so much from the tape recorder but talking to him rather from inside his head. It was Conn Ductor!

"Greetings, Manchild! Much time has passed since you left us. There is a large quantity to tell. When you went, the battle of the Baroque Plains still raged. It continued mercilessly for two full cycles, ceaselessly sounding the clash between Music and Noise. On the third day, it seemed that it would continue until all had been destroyed! I waited for a way to be shown. Then, you helped us once again as you always have. Self-pitying Comm Posor returned to Harmony, whining and weasel-faced, cursing all living things – but mainly I am sorry to relate, cursing you, Manchild!"

Tristan smiled defiantly.

"...After binding Comm Posor with three chains of golden bells, I tied him on the Royal Diatonic Fugue and flew through the skies of Audia to the Baroque Plains. When I reached the scene of violence with my valuable cargo, I could detect that the forces of Noise were growing weaker. But still, it would have gone on. There were heavy losses on both sides and who knows how the final tide might have turned? The noble Prince Crescendo went to the rescue of a stricken Concord. Whilst he was defending him, the evil Baron Dis

Onance rode up behind and dealt him a deadly Din blow – we lost both Crescendo and his steed Pibcorn.

"I cried, 'This must stop!' and, summoning up my power, I sent a white fire-ball blazing with booming Music into the troubled sky. All eyes turned upwards. Once more, 'This must stop!' I cried to them, 'Cacophony is defeated! I hold him chained, helpless behind me. Loud Crashbang, your son, Buzz Deafening is destroyed, his mission a failure. Harmony is stronger than she ever was before. You cannot win now. Music is safe. If you deign to continue this futile struggle, then I shall be forced to unleash my full power against Din.'"

Conn Ductor continued, "Surveying the Discords below with baleful glances, I sent a searing Musical bolt of rainbow fire just above their helmeted and masked heads. All Discords covered their scaly hearing holes and some fell senseless to the ground. It became obvious to them that their wicked plan of conquest had failed; their spirit broke and they laid down their Chaos weapons.The Army of Anxiety, weaponless and disheartened, wended its weary way back to Din. Lord Loud Crashbang will never lead an army out of Din, nor leave Castle Meegrain again. Of that I am sure."

Tristan sighed with relief, though not totally convinced *all* Harmony's troubles were gone for good. Where there's goodness, there's badness; but that's how it is. Yes, darkness lightens sometimes and it is enough that goodness should be stronger.

Music sometimes needs noise, chaos, cacophony, and discords to surprise and reveal a contrast. There is a place for the dark side of music, just as beauty requires ugliness to reveal its true worth, as long as that dark side is kept in its place. But Music is a sort of spirit and never dies.

"There was much celebrating at our victory, Manchild; although Tranquil Queen Rhapsody mourned much over the loss of so many Concords and especially over the passing of the noble Prince Crescendo. Both he and Prince Andante have been made 'Heroes of Harmony' and will have golden statues raised to their names."

Conn Ductor continued, "There was also much sorrow over your absence, Manchild. That brings me to our present concern. We know that the wicked one had taken your tape away when you forced him to return. Unfortunately, when he came back, he no longer had the tape with him. However much I tried, I could not glean from him the secret place where he had hidden it. All I can be sure of is that it must be somewhere in Audia and not Lumio. The problem is, Manchild that the Brio-key was made by Inno Vator many, many years ago. Since his passing, the skill of its creation has been lost. I cannot make another!"

Tristan rubbed his head in a despondent way, holding back feelings of depression at the news. Searching for the tape was like looking for a needle in a haystack. He moaned.

"However," Conn Ductor continued, "all is not lost, for I am using all my power to search our land for the tape and Bop Shoowah, Scherzo, and your good, tireless friend, Princess Melody are assisting me. With their help and my ancient Music books, I have managed to send this message to you. If I can accomplish this, then you must realise it is only a matter of time before I retrieve the tape."

Tristan gazed at the Motown Nuts that Bop Shoowah had given him, seemingly so long ago. 'At least there is hope,' he said, bucking himself up.

"The evil Eye, Aleatoree, is returned once more to the head of Obi in Chaos Desert. I have buried it again, covering it with a pentangle of bells that will prevent any evil-wisher approaching it to unleash its power. As for Comm Poser, I thought it fitting to imprison *him* once more in the great golden bell-room. Any musical sound still weakens him considerably. I have built this bell into my Palace in a tune-sealed chamber, deep in the cellars. I shall keep watch over him. I know the evil and trickery that even now burns within his twisted soul. But through instruction and conditioning, I shall attempt to untwist his soul and bring forth any remnants of good in him to the surface once more.

Conn Ductor continued, "Now, ah yes, Manchild, Scherzo asked me to say that he made a poem for you. I am afraid that it is not awfully good, but take it as you will!"

Tristan, Manchild so bold,
regained the Metronome of Gold
And Cacophony, instead of King,
became once more a captured thing,
Beneath the giant Golden Bell,
alone forever doomed to dwell.
Instead of two worlds complete,
Din's domain became defeat
So, thanks to Tristan, all Concords send:
you are our true and loyal friend!

The poem made Tristan feel happy – like a visit from a great soul-mate you haven't seen for some time.

"But, the prime thing for you, Manchild, is that Tranquil Queen Rhapsody has named you, 'Tristan, Music Keeper of Lumio'! This is an honour of the very first order and is well-deserved by you, Tristan, my boy. When you return, you will be welcomed as a Hero. Meanwhile, you must keep watch in this world. You are our eyes and ears and we are linked by our bond. Keep watch. Keep watch. We will have such celebrations 'when' you return, for never fear, Tristan, return you shall. We will find the Brio-key ... never... fear... goodbye for... now..."

Conn Ductor's voice began to fade away and as it went, so too did the tape, slowly vanishing until there was no trace of it remaining. Tristan switched off the recorder and, getting undressed, he got back into bed and fell asleep. *A world*

161

without music – unimaginable. The conflict between chaos and harmony, good and evil runs through the soul of every man *and woman.*

His worries, doubts, and fears faded – hope, like a child, turned back from the dark and a little man with changing coloured hair said, 'See you soon – see you soon!' over and over again like music in his mind.

Then, when woken by his alarm, Tristan immediately remembered all of his adventures in Audia with the quality of a vivid dream. Its music was firmly with him – in his very soul forever.

Suddenly, he heart his father's voice, "Tristan, son, the twins, Beatrice and Florence are coming to see you. They'll be here mid-day."

"Life makes sense when I am filled with music and this morning," he said, stretching with a smile toward the new sun rising four-square in the sky, "I feel that I can cope with anything!"

If you listen silently enough, you can touch the colour of music and feel the texture of time.

Tristan loved music – any kind of music, any time and, smiling resolutely, he picked up his violin and started to play.

Postlude

So there you have it, the manuscript as written by my uncle.

Yes, quite fanciful, but how much truth does it contain you might wonder. I wonder that too.

I've been having a go on my uncle Tristan's violin, he played professionally you know and was quite renowned.

Anyway, exciting news; the Cassette tape player has come back by courier – and, because you are still here, I want you to witness me playing this tape. So, press open and put the tape in.

Wow...

The tape's clicked into place and, now that I've shut the cover and have pressed play, there is the growing sensation of strange music.

It's the most enchanting tune that I've ever heard, like a wonderfully fresh-scented wind on a warm, close day. It seems to be coming from deep inside of me. Threading and weaving, filling my senses, carrying me away like a dream.

Everything is swaying and fading and something else is taking its place and...

Uncle Tristan...is that you? ... Uncle Tristan....
You look so young.

David R. Morgan

David R Morgan lives in England. He is a full-time teacher and writer. He has written music journalism, poetry, and children's books. He has won awards for his writing; both for fiction and poetry.

For the last five years, he has been working on the Soundings Project with his son, Toby, performing his own poetry and writing to Toby's original music and their self-created video/films. This work is on YouTube, Spotify and Soundcloud.

For over a year, he has been working with Terrie Sizemore and her innovative Florida, USA Publishing House, A2Z Press LLC, writing a variety of picture/story books. It has been an exhilarating experience, which has now led to the revision and publishing of this new novel: *The Magic Tape*. This is what you now have in your hands.

Music and Light - worlds must be balanced. In *The Magic Tape* we discover there is a journey to go on and a battle to be won. Join Tristan and so many incredible characters on this magical adventure as he shifts between two worlds to save them both from darkness, noise, and chaos. Musicians are jugglers. They use harmonies instead of rings and make magic from curving air – such an optimistic thing to do even in the most pessimistic of times!

Lightning Source UK Ltd.
Milton Keynes UK
UKHW011947211220
375665UK00001B/13